THE CHANGE UP

INDIANAPOLIS LIGHTNING SERIES BOOK 4

SAMANTHA LIND

SAMANTHALIND.COM

Cover Design by Jersey Girl Design
Cover image by Wander Aguiar
Cover Model Eddie
Editing by *Amy Briggs ~ Briggs Consulting LLC*
Proofreading by *Proof Before You Publish*

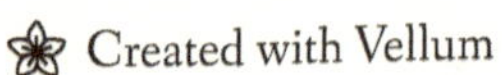 Created with Vellum

CONTENTS

ONE

MATT

I RELAX ON A BEACH CHAIR, SOAKING IN THE HOT sun as I take in my surroundings. The past season was tough; playing professional baseball is starting to take its toll on my body. I glance over at my friend and teammate, Lucas, and his new girlfriend, Carmen, our team's PR manager. The love that radiates off of the two makes me long for that kind of connection with a woman.

I look away, taking in my surroundings on the beach. The water is calling my name, so I get up and head closer to the shoreline. I see a young boy throwing a baseball at a beautiful woman as I approach. The smiles that fill their faces cause one to tug at my lips. The carefree way they play as the water laps at their ankles has me longing for that kind of contentment. For that fulfillment that a wife and kids would bring to my life. At thirty-two, I did not have many years left playing baseball. I've had the time to live the bachelor's life, a wild one, at times, with my profession, but that kind of lifestyle isn't sustainable and isn't how I want the rest of my life to go.

The young boy attempts to toss the ball back to his mother, but he misses as the ball sails my way, landing in front of my feet. I pick it up and walk it a few feet over to them.

"Here ya go, buddy," I say, handing the ball over to the boy.

"Thank you." He smiles up at me, his toothless grin making me chuckle slightly.

"I'm so sorry about that," the woman says. "Not the greatest aim when you're five years old."

"It's no problem, ma'am. I've tossed a few balls in my day; sometimes they go where you want, and some-times they don't."

"Thank you. I've been working with him; he's obsessed with t-ball, but I'm not all that great with it," she says.

"I could give him a few pointers, if you'd like," I offer.

"I wouldn't want to interrupt your vacation," she says, glancing behind me. "I'm sure your wife or girl-friend would want you with them."

"No wife or girlfriend. I'm here with a few friends, more like the third wheel," I find myself telling her. "No pressure or anything; I wouldn't want to step on your husband's toes, either." I noticed a quick flash of pain in her eyes at my last statement and could kick my own ass for obviously bringing up something painful for her.

"If you truly don't mind, then Brayden would love it, I'm sure," she says, smiling up at me.

"Matt," I tell her, holding out a hand. The moment her tiny hand is in mine, an electrical current zings up my arm. She quickly shakes my hand, then drops it, and I have to wonder if she felt the same current.

"Hannah, and this is Brayden," she says before crouching down so she's closer to his height. She places her hands on his shoulders, turning him to face her. "Mr. Matt has offered to give you a few throwing pointers; how does that sound?" she asks him. His face lights up as he starts jumping up and down.

"Yes!" he exclaims, and Hannah and I both laugh at his excitement.

"Do you mind if we move a little further down the beach?" I ask Hannah. "Just over there." I point to a larger open space. "That way, we have room and don't have to worry about hitting anyone."

"Sure, let me grab our stuff," she says. I follow them to a couple of beach chairs. She stuffs a few toys into a bag. I grab the chairs before she can and start heading for the clearing. Once there, I set up the chairs, grab the baseball, and move out ten or so feet in front of them.

"Here, buddy, show me what you've got," I tell Brayden, tossing him the ball. I crouch down, making myself as close to his size as I possibly can, being since I'm over six feet tall. I watch as he pulls his hand back, then releases the ball as his hand passes his shoulder. The ball goes flying, way to the left of me as I go lunging for it. It hits the sand, as does my body.

I toss the ball with Brayden for a good half-hour, maybe even forty-five minutes before he tires out. I've laughed more during our time playing than I probably have in the last few years. "I'm tired. Can we take a break, Mr. Matt?" he asks, walking the ball over to me rather than throwing it.

"Of course, we can," I tell him, dropping my hand to the top of his head and messing up his wind-blown hair. I followed him back to the chairs, where Hannah sat, watching us the entire time. He sits down on her lap, leaving the second chair empty. "Do you mind?" I ask, nodding my head in the direction of the second chair.

"Of course not. Can I offer you something to drink?" she asks. "Actually; I only have water," she corrects. My eyes lock on how she worries her lip, waiting on my answer. My dick hardens at the sight, and I get instant flashes of her lips wrapped around my cock. *Where in the hell did those thoughts come from?*

"Water's great," I tell her, clearing my throat as I'm suddenly thirstier than I should be.

We make small talk for a few minutes, mainly about the resort and pleasant weather.

"I should get going; let the two of you get back to

your vacation," I tell Hannah before standing. I brush off some sand that somehow made it into my lap.

"Thank you for playing with Brayden. That was very kind of you. It was nice to meet you," she says before I can walk away.

"I had fun, and I hope he did, as well." I watch as Hannah cuddles her son against her chest, running her hands through his hair as he watches something on her phone.

"He's definitely going to sleep well tonight, which means I should be able to sleep well tonight, so thank you for that."

"Anytime. I'll be here for a few more days, so if I see y'all out here again, I'll stop by to see if he's up to tossing the ball around again."

"I'm sure he'd love that, but please don't feel like you need to miss out on time with your friends to play ball with him," she tells me.

"Keeps me from being the third wheel. I still don't know why they insisted I come along," I tell her honestly.

"They sound like good friends."

"Some of the best," I tell her, meaning every word.

"Well then, I guess we'll see you around. We also will be here for a few more days."

With that, I take off down the beach, heading towards my room. I need a beer and a nap, not necessarily in that order.

I stop at one of the resort bars just off the wing

where my room is located and order a beer. With the cold bottle in my hand, I make my way down the corridor to my door. After flashing the key card in front of the lock, I push my way inside. I tear off my sandals and rub my feet on the mat to try and get rid of the sand that was stuck to my skin.

I walk further into the room, set my beer down on the nightstand, before I collapse on the bed. I turn the TV on, flipping through the channels, trying to find something that holds my interest. With not much on, I pull my phone out and scroll through the news headlines before getting sucked into TikTok videos.

I startle awake; my vibrating cell on my chest wakes me up as it rings. I wipe a hand over my face before picking the device up and looking at the screen. When I see who's calling, I hit ignore and toss the phone on the bed beside me. It's an old friend with benefits. I haven't heard from her in months, back when she cut things off because she'd met someone and was going to see where that led her. Her calling me now tells me that things didn't work out, and she wants to resume what we had before. Which I'm not interested in right now.

My stomach starts to grumble; a quick glimpse at the clock tells me that it's dinnertime. I get out of bed and head for the bathroom. A quick piss and some water splashed on my face, and I'm awake and ready to take on the night.

Making my way to one of the dining areas the

resort has to offer, I noticed Hannah and Brayden just about to enter, as well. I pick up my speed, catching up to them just after they reach the door.

"Evening," I greet. Hannah's eyes flash to mine, and I can't help but be drawn to them.

"Hi, how was your afternoon?" Hannah asks as we wait in line for the hostess.

"Pretty relaxing. Took a much-needed nap. How was yours?" I ask as we step forward.

"We stayed down at the beach for an hour or so, then went to the pool. We were starving when we got out, so a quick shower and change of clothes, and here we are."

"How many?" the hostess interrupts our conversation.

"Three, please," I say before Hannah can answer. She quirks a brow in question, but doesn't refute my answer. We follow the hostess to a booth, and I wait to let Brayden and Hannah pick a side before I slide in across from them.

"I hope you don't mind having dinner together," I offer as an apology once the hostess walks away.

"It's fine; I don't want to impose on your vacation," she says.

"I wouldn't be here if I didn't want to be."

"Good evening, I'm Beth, and I'll be taking care of you tonight. Can I start anyone off with a beverage? Maybe a cocktail or glass of wine?"

"Can I get a chocolate milkshake, Mom?" Brayden asks. The look of hope is evident on his face.

"We are on vacation, so I guess so." She smiles down at him. "A *small*." I can't help but chuckle at the way she emphasizes the word small to the server. "Chocolate milkshake for my son, and I'll have a lemon drop martini and a glass of ice water, please."

"Would you like whip cream and a cherry on top of the milkshake?" Beth asks.

"Yes!" Brayden answers her, bouncing in his seat.

"I got you, buddy!" Beth tells him, winking at the kid. "And for you, sir?" She turns her attention to me.

"I'll take a blue moon with a slice of orange."

"Would you also like a glass of water?" she asks.

"Sure, that'd be great," I tell her.

"Did you want any appetizers, or do you need a minute to look over the menu?" she asks.

"Can we get some of the pretzel bites and the mozzarella sticks?" Hannah asks.

"Sure can; I'll get them put in right away," Beth says before stepping away from our table.

"He's going to get hangry soon, so I figured some easy appetizers were a good start," she tells me as she fidgets with the edges of her menu.

"It's all good," I tell her, hoping that she catches on to my calm demeanor.

I take my time checking out the menu. This isn't one of the fancy restaurants that the resort has, more like a diner or national chain back home. They have a mixture of just about everything; steaks, pasta, burgers, tacos. My mouth waters as I read over everything, making it hard to decide what I want to get.

"Do you know what you're getting?" Hannah asks a few minutes later.

"I think the brisket tacos, what about you?"

"The shrimp scampi with extra shrimp," she says just as our server returns with our drinks. I can't help but smirk when she sets the shake glass down in front of Brayden. The thing is enormous and topped with probably three inches of whip cream covered with sprinkles and a cherry on top.

"Sorry, this is the only size we offer," Beth says apologetically.

"It's okay," Hannah says as she laughs it off. I can't help but be impressed at how easygoing she is taking it. I know some parents who'd blow a gasket over it, but she's as cool as a cucumber.

"I guess that's the beauty of vacation; we can eat ice cream for dinner, if we want," I chime in.

"Guess so," Hannah agrees.

"Are you ready to order?" Beth asks. "The apps should be up in a moment."

"I think we are," Hannah says, looking to me to confirm. I nod my agreement and let Hannah order for the two of them before I give Beth my order.

"How long have you been here?" Hannah asks once Beth has left our table.

"Just got here this morning. Took the red-eye flight last night. How about you?"

"We got here a few days ago, so we've had time to explore and have fun."

"And how long will you be here?" I ask.

"Another couple days," she answers. "And you?"

"Four days," I tell her. "Are you here celebrating anything special, or just a week away from the hustle and bustle of life?"

That same flash of pain that I noticed when we were on the beach quickly passed through her eyes. She looks over at Brayden and runs her hand through his hair. He's busy trying to figure out the maze puzzle on the kids' menu.

"This time of year is always hard for us; my husband passed away three years ago this week," she says, looking back my way.

"I'm so sorry for your loss," I tell her, now understanding the flashes of pain I noticed.

"Thank you; it was a sudden car accident," she says. "Each year gets slightly easier. Brayden and I left town the week of the first anniversary, and it was the best spur-of-the-moment decision I ever made. After that trip, I've planned a vacation for us each year."

"Making good memories to overshadow the sad ones sounds like a good idea," I say, not sure if it is the right thing, actually, to say.

"Yeah, I also like being away, just the two of us. It helps us unplug and not be available for all the people who are trying to be nice by checking in on the anniversary of his death to make sure we're doing okay. Sometimes getting all those messages all at once makes it hard to breathe, hard to cope, and function. But by being gone and unplugged, I can control when and if I even look at them. Absorb them in small amounts when I'm ready for them."

"Makes perfect sense."

"What about you? Are you here celebrating anything special?"

"Not really, just needed to get away," I tell her.

I hold back the information that I'm a baseball player, and it's the offseason, so this is my time to relax and recharge before the grueling season starts again when we report to camp in February. I like the idea that she has no clue—or, at least, hasn't suggested she knows—I'm Matt O'Riley, star first baseman for the Indianapolis Lightning.

TWO
HANNAH

I SIT ACROSS THE TABLE FROM MATT, STILL A little apprehensive about this man, yet also finding myself very smitten with him. The way he played with Brayden on the beach, showing him how to throw the baseball, melted my mom's heart all the way. As much as I miss Ryan and always will, the one thing I hate the most is that Brayden is missing out on growing up with his dad. Learning all the things that Ryan dreamed about teaching him. We'd talked at great length when I was pregnant about all the things he couldn't wait to do with our son. All the trips and experiences he was so ready to have and bond over. Brayden was only two when Ryan died, so they didn't accomplish many. I also hate the fact that Brayden doesn't really remember Ryan. He recognizes him in pictures that I keep around the house and knows things about him that family or friends have told him, but he doesn't remember him from his own memories from when Ryan was alive.

I shake out of my thoughts, not wanting to zone out during dinner.

"I've got your appetizers for you," Beth says, setting down the two plates I'd ordered. Brayden immediately reaches over to grab a mozzarella stick, dipping it into the marinara sauce so hard that it sloshes over the side of the ramekin.

"Brayden!" I scold. "Please be careful."

"Sorry," he says, slinking back against the booth.

"It's okay, buddy," Matt tells him, and he perks right back up. "I've made bigger messes in my life; just be careful going forward."

"Do you have kids? You're so good around them," I ask.

"Nope. Some of my best friends and coworkers have kids that are around when we get together after work," he says.

"You're a natural and will make a good dad someday," I tell him, believing every word of my statement. Some people are just naturals when it comes to kids, and the few interactions I've seen of Matt with Brayden makes me think he's one of them wholeheartedly.

We fall into a comfortable silence as we devour the appetizers while we wait on our main course to arrive. We exchange a few small talk questions, getting to know each other better as we share the meal.

I haven't had the urge to get back out there in the dating world, but sitting across from this man has my mind racing. The way he so readily accepts both Brayden and me is reassuring. It makes me have a sliver of hope that there are good men out there and that one day I might find love again. Being a widowed single mother can be lonely. I know Ryan would want me to move on and find someone to take care of us; I don't know what I'm doing when it comes to dating. Ryan and I were high school sweethearts. He was my first everything, and I thought he would be my last. But life happens, and I've grown and learned from it to the best of my ability.

"THANKS FOR LETTING ME HAVE DINNER WITH THE two of you tonight. It beat sitting by myself," Matt says as we go to exit the restaurant.

"Anytime," I tell him, meaning it. "Didn't you say you came with some friends?" I ask.

"I did, Lucas and Carmen," he says.

"Won't they expect you to have dinner with them?" I ask.

"I'm sure I'll meet up with them at some point while we're here, but I'd prefer not to be the third wheel, as much as possible. They're still in the new relationship, honeymoon, can't keep their hands off of each other, phase, and I'd like to be spared the PDA," he tells me.

"Ah, not one for all the lovey-dovey stuff?" I teasingly ask.

"If it was me, sure, but when I have to look at it all the time, no." He grins down at me. I swear, his smile does something to my insides. I didn't notice it earlier, but there's definitely something about this man that has my body on alert.

"What are you doing for the rest of the evening?" I ask as we walk down the corridor that leads outside to the courtyard area that sits between the main resort building and the beach.

"Hadn't decided yet. I was kind of thinking of walking out and finding a spot to listen to the waves and checking out the stars. What about the two of you?" he asks.

"Brayden wanted to do the movie at the pool."

"That sounds like fun; what are they showing?" he asks.

"I believe tonight is *Sing*."

"Never heard of it," he says.

"It's pretty cute. An animated movie with singing and dancing animals."

"Interesting," he muses. "Might have to come check it out."

"You're welcome to join us. Brayden will probably be in the pool the entire time, and I'll be on a lounge chair. They set out popcorn and other snacks, plus have the pool bar open."

"They really do think of everything around here."

"They do. This has been just what we needed this week," I tell him honestly. I've already shared about Ryan, and Matt makes me feel so comfortable, so I don't mind opening up to him a little.

"What time does it start?" he asks, looking down at the watch on his wrist. I hadn't noticed it before, but it seems expensive. It makes me wonder what he does for a living.

"I think around eight. I know after sundown."

"Perfect, I'll meet you there. Save me a seat?" he asks.

"Sure," I agree before he takes off.

"ARE YOU READY TO HEAD DOWN TO THE POOL?" I ask Brayden. We came back to our room after parting ways with Matt. Got in a little downtime and gave us time to change into our bathing suits. I put mine on but also pulled out my coverup. I don't plan on getting into the water unless I absolutely need to.

"Yes!" he exclaims.

He's excited he gets to stay up late and eat junk that we only do for special occasions at home. Keeping a strict schedule at home is necessary. It helps keep me sane in all the chaos.

"Let's go, then." I laugh at his antics. The way he jumps all around. We slip our sandals on, I grab my pool bag, and we head out the door.

I'm surprised when we get down to the pool and I find Matt already there, three lounge chairs pulled together with a bucket of popcorn already sitting on each of them.

"Hi," I greet as we approach.

"Hey, I was bored, so I headed down early. Is this okay?" he asks, pointing to the seats.

"It's perfect," I tell him, catching myself smiling up at him again.

I set my bag down on one of the chairs. "Do you want to sit down with us and have some popcorn or get into the pool?" I ask Brayden. "You can't have the popcorn in the pool," I remind him.

He looks between the chair with popcorn and the water a few times. "I'll sit first." He plops down on the chair, shoving a handful of popcorn into his mouth.

"Good option," Matt tells him, messing his already messy hair.

We all take our seats, and I end up in the middle. While we aren't touching at all, I find the proximity to Matt intoxicating. I don't know where this desire has come from, but I find myself wishing he'd lean over and kiss me or hold my hand. I haven't felt this desire since Ryan was alive, and that scares the shit out of me.

We sit back, popcorn buckets in hand, and watch as the movie starts. I can't help but attempt to sneak glances Matt's way. I love the way his face lights up when he laughs at the movie. It really is a cute movie. He catches me looking his way a couple of times, winking at me just now. I can feel the blush heat my cheeks after being caught.

Brayden decides about halfway through the movie to go get into the water. He finds a tube so he can sit up comfortably to watch the movie.

With him out of earshot, Matt leans closer to me, and my heart kicks up a few beats per minute. He's close enough I can smell his cologne. "Can I take you out, just the two of us, tomorrow night?"

I mull over his question for a few moments before turning to stare at him. The look of desire written all over this man's face has heat pooling in my belly and my center clenching.

"I'd love that," I tell him honestly. "I'll have to check with the kids club, if they have a spot open for tomorrow night, but as long as they do, then yes, I'd love to go to dinner with you."

I catch a flash of dimples the way he smiles at my answer. Dimples are my kryptonite, so I'm really in for it now.

"I might have asked at the concierge desk when I was making reservations for dinner tomorrow night and they already have him booked in. I wanted all my bases covered if you agreed to the date."

I'm speechless. The fact this man took it upon himself to make sure my son was taken care of first, says so much about him. "Thank you," I whisper, doing my damnedest to hold back the tears that want to fall.

"Of course, I knew that Brayden couldn't be on his own, so I took care of his needs, first."

"You really are one of a kind," I tell him as I pat his hand. He quickly turns his hand to capture mine and brings it up to his lips, placing a kiss on my fingers.

"Just being myself. I can't help it that I've met the most beautiful woman I've ever had the pleasure of spending time with while on a vacation. Got to make the most of our time together."

"Charmer," I tease him, pulling away before I do something crazy like kiss him with my kid just a few feet away.

"If you like charming, I can make sure to charm you tomorrow night." He smirks.

"I'm sure you can," I tell him as I turn to check on Brayden. He's moving toward the edge, getting himself out. I can tell he's getting tired as he makes his way back over to us. "Are you tired, buddy?" I ask him.

"A little," he says, yawning as he sits down on Matt's seat.

"Want to lay here and watch the rest?" Matt asks him as he opens up his arms. Brayden climbs right up into Matt's lap, snuggling into him the way a little boy would do with his dad. It breaks my heart just a little, but also makes my heart so happy. The way that Brayden has taken to Matt is incredible. I just need to be careful that he doesn't get too attached to this man.

We'll be parting ways in just a days, all going back to our normal lives.

"That didn't take long," I muse, peering over at Brayden a few minutes later. He's sound asleep in Matt's arms.

"I figured he'd crash; it was one of the reasons I offered for him to climb up. Figured, this way, he's already in my arms so I can carry him back to your room for you."

"You really do think of everything."

"Like I said, I've been around enough of my friends' kids to know the signs. My friend Derek has a few little girls. They like to have everyone over to their house for summer barbecues. Once the girls come out of the pool and the sun goes down, they usually crash in whoever's lap they've climbed up into. It has happened to me more times than I can count."

"Sounds like some fun times, and you've got quite the friend group."

"I did luck out when it came to my friends," he admits.

I gather our stuff, putting the popcorn buckets all together for the staff to collect, along with our trash so it's easy for them to take.

"You're sure you don't mind carrying him back for me?" I ask as I stand, sliding my sandals on.

"Something tells me that he's getting a little big for you to carry," Matt smirks.

"That he is, but I make do when needed," I tell

him. "No other choice, really."

"I've got him, you lead the way," he insists. I wait a moment while he stands up, making sure he isn't going to lose his balance and drop my baby. Once I'm satisfied that he's got him, I lead the way to our room. I splurged slightly by getting a suite, not one of the multi-room ones, but a little larger than the standard hotel room.

We quietly enter the room. I toss my bag on the floor and walk over to the second bed, pulling the sheets back so Matt can place Brayden directly into bed. "Is this good?" he asks, and I nod my approval.

I touch him to make sure he isn't wet still from the pool, which I find he isn't. Once Matt leaves, I can slip him out of his swim trunks and into some underwear and PJs.

"Thank you again," I tell him. "What time do I need to be ready tomorrow?" I ask him.

"I made reservations for six. Brayden's reservation in the kids club starts at five, and they'll feed him dinner," he tells me as we step closer to the door.

"Thank you," I tell him, still a little dumbfounded this man has taken care of everything.

"See you tomorrow," he says before reaching for the door. I watch as he retreats down the hall. I can't help but take in his muscular form, the way his ass fills out the shorts he's got on, and the way his biceps push the limits of his T-shirt. Add in the scruff on his face and I'm ready to melt in this man's presence.

THREE
MATT

I took a gamble when I booked reservations for the steakhouse and the kids club for Brayden. Thank fuck that gamble paid off when Hannah said yes to a date. From the moment I saw her across the beach, I've been drawn to her. I can't explain it, I just am.

I run a towel across my head, soaking up some water from my shower. I squirt a little bit of gel into my palm, rubbing my hands together before I run them through my hair. Once I'm satisfied with my hair, I pull out my electric razor, cleaning up the facial hair just a little bit.

Once done in the bathroom, I head out into the bedroom, stopping at the closet where I pick from the clothes I brought with me. I'm glad that I decided to toss in a few nicer polos and shorts, in the off chance that I ended up at the steakhouse for dinner. Before coming here, I'd have figured that would have been with Carmen and Lucas, but here I am about to go out on a date. Something I haven't done in a long-ass time. I'm feeling a little rusty at this whole dating thing, so hopefully, I don't fuck it up and make an ass out of myself tonight.

I finally pick a pair of navy shorts and a turquoise polo. Once dressed, I stop in the bathroom one last time to spray on some cologne and make sure I'm presentable. Satisfied I'm good, I head for Hannah's room. We're down different wings, but I make it to hers within a few minutes.

I suck in a deep breath before I rap my knuckles against the door. I'd talked to the concierge desk this morning and arranged for some outfits to be sent to her room for her to choose from for tonight. I want her to feel like a princess. If I'm only awarded one night with this woman, I want to make the most of it.

"Coming," I hear her call out from the other side. I can't help but chuckle as I imagine her trying to put on shoes or something as she hops to the door.

She opens the door and I about swallow my tongue. "Hi," she shyly says, giving me a slight wave as she stands next to the open door.

"Fuck, you're gorgeous," I tell her, stepping closer. I want to kiss the fuck out of this woman, but I hold back. I don't know where her head is at, and I don't want to do anything that makes her uncomfortable.

"You clean up pretty nice yourself," she says.

"Is this one of the outfits that were sent up?" I ask, needing to talk so I don't throw caution to the wind and just take her to bed.

"It is," she confirms. "And thank you for doing that. You definitely didn't have to."

"I wanted this to be a special night for you."

"Well, you've succeeded, and the night hasn't even started."

"Shall we?" I ask, gesturing for her to exit the room and walk in front of me.

Hannah walks out of the room, stopping to make sure the door closes all the way. I place a hand at the small of her back as we walk down the corridor. The steakhouse is located upstairs in the main building. It is small and intimate. All the tables are next to the floor-to-ceiling windows that give you amazing views of the water and sunset.

"Good evening, do you have reservations?" the hostess asks as we approach.

"We do, for two at six. Under Matt," I tell her.

"Of course, right this way," she says after checking the computer. She leads us to a table tucked in its own little semi-private corner. When I booked, I asked for something like this. I haven't been recognized yet, but I don't want tonight to be the night that I am. I'm liking the anonymity I've had so far this trip.

As soon as we're seated, the server is at our table, giving us the rundown of the menu, along with the specials, including their wine pairings.

Once we've had a few moments to view the menu, we put in our orders. I notice Hannah wavering over the drink menu. "Order anything you'd like, I promise I'll get you home tonight." I wink at her, hoping to help calm her nerves.

She nibbles at her bottom lip and my shorts get a little snugger. "I'll have the daiquiri flight sample," she tells our server.

"Good choice," he says, tapping at his tablet. "It will be just a few minutes for your appetizers, and I'll be right back with your drinks. Please don't hesitate to flag any of us down if you need anything before then."

"Thank you," I tell him before he steps away.

"Was Brayden excited to go to the kids club?" I ask, reaching for my water glass.

"He was so excited. Made me walk him down around four-thirty, so he wouldn't miss a minute of his time there. They weren't full, so they let him come in early, which was nice as it gave me a few extra minutes to get ready."

"I'm glad that he was excited for it. What did you do today?"

"After room service breakfast, we went on a boat tour out to one of the island beaches. We had lunch out there, which was incredible. If you have time to do one, I highly recommend it. Then, we came back and had some downtime in the room. Took a short nap, and just cuddled together until it was time to drop him off. How about you?"

"I met up with my friends for brunch late morning. Then, we hung out at the pool for a while. A pretty relaxing day."

"Sounds perfect," she muses just as our server appears with our drinks. He sets the flight of four small glasses down in front of Hannah with four different colored daiquiris and a beer in front of me.

"I'll be right back with your appetizers," he says before retreating again.

"Cheers," I say, picking up my beer and holding it up for her to clink one of her glasses with. She picked the first one, a red-colored drink.

"Cheers." She clinks her glass and I watch as she takes a drink of the icy liquid. I'm jealous of the straw she wraps her lips around, wishing it was my cock she was wrapping them around. Once again, I find my shorts getting snugger as the evening goes on. By the time our meal comes, I'm not sure if I'll have any more room in them. Thank God for the table-cloths helping to hide the bulge I'm sporting right now.

"CAN I TEMPT EITHER OF YOU WITH SOME dessert?" our server asks once all our dishes have been removed from the table.

"What do you say?" I ask Hannah.

"I don't know, I'm not sure I can take another bite,

but some of the items were calling my name earlier," she says.

"Go ahead and bring us the menu, we can always take it with us."

"Of course, I'll be right back," he says, stepping away and grabbing the dessert menu. He hands both of us a copy. I glance over it quickly, not really picky as they all sound delicious. I watch as Hannah mulls over the menu. The small facial changes as she reads over each option and their ingredients.

"Anything calling your name?" I ask.

"All of it," she chuckles, and I can't help but join her.

"We can get one of each and take them with us. We might end up in a sugar coma, but at least we'd be able to say we'd tried them all."

"I'd be so sick." She laughs. "How about the crème brûlée or the cheesecake? That is, if you're willing to share one with me."

"How about we get one of each and we can share both?" I suggest.

"Now that I can do," she agrees.

Our server returns and I put in our order, the crème brûlée for here and the cheesecake to go.

He returns quickly with the items, placing two spoons down with the dessert between us. I crack the hard topping of sugar, scooping a spoonful of the dessert up. I hold the spoon out to Hannah, offering her the first bite. She hesitates for a half-second before leaning forward and taking the bite I'm offering. I thought I was jealous of the straw earlier, now I can add a fucking spoon to that list.

"Hmmm," she moans as the dessert hits her taste-buds. My cock doesn't know that she's moaning at the food, all it knows is the gorgeous woman is moaning within his proximity and I'm harder than I've ever been.

"Hannah," I huskily say her name. "You're killing me here," I warn her. Her cheeks instantly go beet red, and all I want to do is strip her bare and watch the rest of her body go red as I make her come.

"Sorry." She squeaks and covers her face.

"Don't hide from me," I say, pulling her hands down from her face. "You're beautiful, and I like seeing you blush."

"I don't know what to say to that," she admits. "I'm —" She hesitates a little, letting the words die on the end of her tongue. "I have no idea what I'm doing. I haven't been on a date in years. My husband was the only man I ever dated, the only man that I ever did *anything* with, so to say I'm so out of my league is an understatement."

"You have nothing to worry about. We take this at your pace. I won't lie to you; I'm extremely attracted to you. I'd take you back to my room right now and rock both of our worlds for whatever amount of time we have together, but I'd be content with just walking along the beach with you, as well."

"Yes," she says, looking me straight in the eye. I hesitate for a moment, making sure I've heard her correctly.

"Yes, what? I need you to spell it out for me, Hannah," I tell her.

"I'm tired of not being spontaneous. It's my last night here, take me back to your room," she says.

I push my chair back and stand up. I help her from her chair and grab the to-go bag. I reach into my back pocket and pull out my wallet, tossing a few hundred bucks on the table as a tip. The restaurant is included since we're at an all-inclusive, but tips are always appreciated by the waitstaff.

I grab her hand, linking our fingers together as we quickly make our way out of the restaurant. I force myself to only hold her hand. If I touch her any more before we reach my room, I can't say that things won't turn X-rated before we're truly alone.

It feels like it takes an hour to make it to my door, when really it only took a few minutes. Before I unlock the door, I spin Hannah until her back is pressed against it and I've got her pinned between it and my body. I run a fingertip down her cheek, hooking it under her chin and tipping her face up. "You are in control. If at any time you want to stop, just say the word and we stop."

"Okay," she says, reaching out and fisting my polo in her hand. She pulls me closer. "Kiss me, Matt."

I don't need to be told twice. I do as the lady

instructs and I bring my lips to hers. Soft, at first. I swipe my tongue along them, tasting remnants of the crème brûlée and rum from her daiquiris.

She opens to me, and our tongues tangle together as we both fight to explore one another. I break the kiss momentarily to unlock the door, taking this inside my room. I pick her up, carrying her over the threshold, and kicking the door closed behind us. I reach back, flipping the lock for assurance that no one is getting in without my approval.

I walk into the room, heading for the bedroom in my suite. I place her down at the foot of the bed, sliding my hands down her curves as I do. They are divine in this dress, but I'd rather see them without anything covering them.

I can tell she's nervous. Not that she has any reason to be, but I get it. This has to be a big moment and decision for her to make. I'm just the lucky bastard that gets this moment in time with her.

"Can I help you out of your dress?" I ask.

"Yes," she says as she moves her hair over a shoulder and turns to show me her back. I grasp the zipper pull and slide it down her back, exposing her creamy skin. I can't help but bring my lips to the exposed skin of her neck as the dress starts to slide down her body as it loosens the further the zipper opens.

"Mhmmm," she moans as I suck at her skin. It puckers under my attention, which spurs me on even more. I want every moan I can get to fall from her lips.

Once I've got the zipper fully open, Hannah shimmies her hips as she pushes the dress down until it drops at our feet. She steps out of it, reaching down to pick it up. I take it from her, tossing it toward the chair in the corner of the room.

Now that she's facing me again, I get my first look at her in the lingerie the store sent up along with the dresses. "Fucking gorgeous," I say as I trace along the top edge of the lace of the bra cups. I can see her pebbled nipples as they push against the thin material. "Lay back on the bed for me," I instruct, and watch as she does just that. I pull the bottom of my polo from my shorts, then up and over my head. I don't miss the way her eyes widen when she sees my bare torso. I undo my shorts, letting them drop to the floor, as well, leaving me in just my briefs. My cock is swollen and hard, making quite the outline on the thin material that is pulled tight thanks to my current status. I chuckle when Hannah's eyes drop quickly down, to check out what I have to offer below the belt. I thought her eyes were wide before, but that was before she got the view she has now.

I crawl onto the bed, hovering over her as she glances up at me. "Like what you see?" I ask.

"Um, yeah," she says breathily. I can't help but chuckle lightly as I bring my lips to hers once again. This kiss is instantly frantic and deep. Her hands find purchase all over my body as they map and explore my exposed skin. She's even brave enough finally to cup my cock in her hand, giving it a quick squeeze before she retreats back to my abs and back up to my biceps.

As much as I'm loving her mouth on mine, I have a soul-deep desire to taste this woman everywhere. I want her to fall apart on my tongue, so I set out to make that happen. I kiss down her neck, meanwhile, reaching behind her and flicking the clasp open. I remove the bra, giving me full access to her pert breasts. They're the perfect handful, with dark pink nipples that are just calling my name. I flick her nipples with my tongue a few times, alternating between the two before picking one to suck into my mouth. The way her body moves beneath me spurs me on, as do the moans that fall from her beautiful lips.

I push down further, nipping and sucking my way down her torso. I kiss along the small scar that sits just above her pubic bone. I'm guessing this is from a c-section, but now's not the time to ask. I glance up to make sure she's still good. "Can I take these off?" I ask, running my finger under the elastic of her panties.

"Yes," she says, nodding enthusiastically. I chuckle at her before I place a kiss on the top of her mound. Her enthusiasm turns to mewls and moans as I slide the thin fabric off her hips and down her legs. I toss them over my shoulder, not really caring where they go.

I slide a finger down her center, pushing her folds

open and exposing her clit. I lightly blow on it and love the way her body arches my direction. I bring my tongue to her, lapping her folds before wrapping my lips around that bundle of nerves. It only takes one hard suck, and her thighs are clenching around my head as she comes. I don't let up as she rides my tongue as her orgasm takes over. Once her legs go limp, I pull back, glancing up at her flushed body as she lays on the bed. "That's one," I tell her, and slide my fingers through her wet folds. I insert two fingers inside her pussy, loving the tightness as she clenches around my fingers. I slowly pump in and out, finding an easy rhythm as I build her up to another orgasm. As soon as I feel her body start to pulse around my fingers, I latch back on to her clit, sending her soaring over the edge.

Once back in limp status, I pull my fingers from her and place kisses on the inside of both of her thighs before I push up the bed to lay next to her. I squeeze my cock, willing it to wait his turn. I reach over to the nightstand and pull out a box of condoms, opening the box and pulling a couple out.

"Can I be on top?" Hannah asks out of the blue.

"You can be wherever you want, sweetheart," I tell her, rolling onto my back. I slip my hands behind my head, giving her however much time she needs. I watch her as she reaches for a condom. I take the hint that she's ready for more and slip my briefs off my hips, tossing them into the pile on the floor with the rest of my clothes. She gasps when she gets a good look at my fully erect cock. I'm not porno huge, but I'd like to think I've got an above-average cock.

"I-I don't think that's going to fit," she says, her eyes wide.

"It will, we'll just take it slow," I assure her.

Hannah finishes opening the condom and tentatively rolls it down my cock. Once it is fully on, she gives my cock a few strokes and I have to think of the dirtiest locker room I can bring up to keep myself from coming right this second.

She slides her leg over my body, straddling my hips. She slides her wet pussy over my cock a few times and all I want to do is slam my cock inside her sweet pussy and come. But I can't do that right now, so I run stats in my mind as I pull her down for a kiss.

We're deep in a kiss when I feel her lift her hips up, my cock lining up with her warm entrance. She slowly sinks down, my girth stretching her walls out as she pushes down until I'm fully seated inside her body. My eyes roll into the back of my head at the feeling. I can only describe this moment as feeling as if I'm home. Where I've always belonged.

"Holy shit," she cries, breaking the kiss. I'm immediately worried. Worried that we've taken things too far, too fast, or that I've somehow hurt her. That is, until she starts to move her hips. Slowly, at first, building up her pace and rhythm. I move my hands to her hips, helping her as she lifts and falls on my cock. She slows, whimpering as she does, so I help her out, bringing my hips up to meet her. I can already feel my balls tingling so I know my orgasm is knocking on the door, but I won't come until she does.

"Matt," she cries. "I'm almost there, I just need more," she tells me. I make a quick decision and flip us over. I bring her heels up to my shoulders, pin her to the bed with my body and fuck her hard and fast. Our bodies are a sweaty mess when she cries out as her orgasm crashes over her, pulling mine from me as she convulses around my cock. I slam inside her one last time, feeling as the tip of the condom fills with my release. I've used every last ounce of my energy, and I collapse on the bed, doing my best not to crush her as her legs wrap around my hips.

"Give me thirty and we can do that again," I tell her a few moments later, once I've had the chance to catch my breath again. I finally pull out of her, rolling out of bed, and head for the bathroom. I take care of the condom before grabbing a washcloth. I run it under warm water, then fill a glass with some cool water, taking them back to the bed, and offering both to Hannah. "If this is our only night together, let's make the most of it."

FOUR

HANNAH

FOUR WEEKS LATER

I stare down at the bathroom counter, too nervous to look at the test that also sits on the counter, just under a washcloth that I covered it with. My timer startles me, telling me my three minutes are up and it's time to learn my fate. I can't believe I'm even in this position. I have sex one fucking time since Ryan died, and here I am, taking a test to see if I'm pregnant.

I take a deep breath, pull up my big girl panties, and move the washcloth. I stare at the digital screen and fall to the floor. *Pregnant.*

What in the hell am I going to do? A single mother already, and now I'm pregnant with a man I don't even really know's baby. A man that I spent a few incredible days with, but realize I don't even know his last name, or where he lives.

Hannah: Are you busy? I have a little emergency and I need you ASAP.
Courtney: I can be over in 20, need me to bring anything?
Hannah: Nope, I just need you.
Courtney: On my way!

God, I love my best friend. She's actually my sister-in-law, but we were friends before I started dating her brother in high school. She has been by my side and my rock since Ryan died. I truly don't know where I'd be without her these last few years.

I pace around the living room and kitchen while I wait on Courtney to arrive. I told her some of what happened on my vacation, but not everything. I guess that will have to change, as of today.

"Mommy, can you open this for me?" Brayden asks.

"What do we say?" I ask him, reminding him to use his manners.

"Please," he replies, handing me his cheese stick. I peel the wrapper open and hand him the cheese.

"Thank you," he says sweetly. I pull him into a hug, tears pricking the back of my eyes as I hold him tight. What in the world am I going to tell him? How do I explain to my five-year-old that mommy got pregnant after a one-night stand on vacation with a man whom she doesn't even know his last name?

"I love you, buddy," I tell him, placing a kiss on the top of his head.

"Love you, too, Mommy," he says before pulling from my embrace and going back to his Lego table.

I watch him for a few minutes, willing the time to pass until Courtney gets here.

"Auntie Court is in da house!" I hear her call out as the door opens.

"Auntie Court!" Brayden yells, and takes off for the front door. He jumps into her arms, wrapping his little body around hers.

"Have you been a good boy for Mommy?" she asks him, rubbing her nose to his. Something they've done since he was a newborn.

"Yes!" he tells her enthusiastically. "Are you coming to my concert this week?" he asks.

"I wouldn't miss it for the world," she assures him before setting him down.

He takes off, going back to the Legos he was working on before she arrived.

"So," she says, dragging out the word as her attention turns to me. "What is the drop-everything-emergency?"

I blow out a huge breath, not really sure how I'm going to get the words past my lips.

"Come on, Han, there isn't anything you could tell me that would shock me. Well, maybe if you said you were pregnant."

My eyes go to the size of saucers at her comment.

"Holy shit." She spells out each letter, the look of shock that covers her face probably matches my own. "Okay, so we've got some talking to do. I guess grabbing a glass of wine first isn't an option, so sit and spill," she instructs.

I lead her into my bedroom. Sitting on my bed, I hold a pillow in front of me, almost like armor.

"Do you remember how I told you about Matt, the guy I met while on vacation?" I ask.

"Yeah, the one that was super amazing with Brayden and who took you out on the romantic date," she says, summarizing the details I did share with her already.

"Right, well, there was more to our date," I confess.

"I guess so." She smiles and bounces her eyebrows at me. "Was the sex good, at least?" she asks.

"Of course, you'd want to know that." I laugh, and it feels good at this moment. "It was amazing. I'm not going to compare Matt and Ryan, because eww, but I can't even form words to explain the night we had together. I don't know if it was because it's been so long or because it was a first for me—being with someone other than Ryan—but it was just amazing. He was so attentive. Kept making sure I was good with everything, he'd stop and remind me that I was in control and if I wasn't okay with something that we'd stop, no questions asked."

"He sounds amazing," she agrees.

"It was truly a special night," I agree. "But

what do I do?" I ask. "I have the man's first name and that is it. I don't know where he lives, what his last name is. Nothing. How in the hell do I go about tracking him down and finding him?" I rapid fire throw out all these questions to Courtney.

"That is a damn good question. We could hire a PI. I'm sure a good one could track down his information from the resort. Do you remember what his room number was? Maybe the hotel will give you his last name or contact information if you call and tell them the situation."

"Maybe." I mull over her suggestions. "If, and I mean a huge *if,* I find him, what am I supposed to do? Show up on his doorstep and say surprise! I'm pregnant with your child, do you want to be involved in the kid's life?"

"I think you're overthinking it. While I agree it is definitely a unique situation, the two of you obviously hit it off. Maybe this is your second chance to fall in love. Just think, if you find him and things work out between the two of you, you'll be living out one of our favorite book tropes." Courtney is doing her damnedest to cheer me up now that I've found my life in shambles.

"I just don't know what I'm going to do." I flop back on the bed, lying on my back as I stare up at the ceiling.

"When did you find out?" she asks.

"About thirty seconds before I texted you," I tell her.

"Oh shit, so you haven't even had time to really process this."

"Exactly. I was feeling off the last few days. My breasts have been killing me. I figured I was getting ready to start my period, so I didn't think anything of it. But as the days went on and the pain got worse and my period never showed up, I started doing the math and realized I'm late. So, a quick stop at Target to grab a few things, I came straight home and peed on the test."

"Damn. Well, congratulations. We'll get through this, whether we find the elusive Matt or not. This baby will be loved and cared for," she assures me.

"You really are the best," I tell her as I pull her into a hug. I let the tears free, crying on her shoulder. We've been in this exact position more times than I can count in the last three years. Each time strengthens our bond.

"Want me to contact the resort?" she asks once my tears have stopped flowing.

"That's probably our first option, not that I expect them to release any information to us, but it doesn't hurt to call and ask. Maybe someone will take pity on my situation and give me what we need."

"Exactly, and if that doesn't work, I can start some research on a good PI."

"I can't believe I have to consider hiring a private investigator," I groan.

"Let me see what I can dig up in the next day or

two and we can go from there. You didn't happen to get any pictures of him, did you?" she asks.

"I don't think so," I tell her, but reach for my phone anyways. Maybe there's one with something that would help. I pull up the pictures from that time, scanning through them quickly. The only one that he's in, you can't see his face at all. It was from when he was throwing the ball with Brayden out on the sand. "Nothing that will help in our search," I tell her, showing her the only picture.

"That's okay, we can do this. We'll figure it all out. Thankfully, you have time to dig and find him before the baby will be here. I'll work on tracking him down, you work on getting an appointment scheduled with your OB and we'll figure the rest out as it comes our way."

"You really do know how to talk me off a ledge," I tell her. "But can we please keep this between the two of us, for now?"

"Of course. I'll be there when you're ready to spill the beans. Before that, my lips are sealed."

"Thanks," I tell her as my stomach does a little roll, and not in a good way. I suck in a deep breath, willing myself to not puke. I haven't gotten sick yet, so this is definitely something new I'm experiencing.

"You, okay? You look a little green," Courtney says.

"Yeah, just my stomach rolling on me. But I'm better now," I assure her. "It just hit me out of nowhere."

"I think that's a sign that you need to eat," she says.

"I probably do; I skipped breakfast this morning," I realize. Thinking back over what I've had - or in this case, haven't had so far today.

"Want to go out to eat or I can make you something quick," she asks.

"I don't really feel like leaving the house again today, but we can order in if you don't want to cook."

"I guess the better question is, what do you want? And do you have anything for me to cook?"

"I have stuff out to make manicotti."

"Yum, let's go make that," she says, hopping off my bed and pulling me with her.

Once we're both standing, she pulls me in for another hug. "Everything will work itself out, I promise."

I'd really like to know where she gets her confidence. I fret over every little thing. It got really bad after Ryan died, but many hours in my therapist's chair have helped me work through my issues.

I pick up the ball, rolling it in my hand. The weight of a baseball feels so natural in my grasp. I've been picking them up for so long, it's all second nature to me. I find the laces with my fingertips, rotating the ball until it is perfect in my grip. I'd been a pitcher in some of my early years, thought I'd continue that path until my high school coach said he needed me to play first base. That changed the trajectory of my career from that moment forward. I made the all-state team my freshman year as I flourished in my new position. I still get the occasional bug to pitch, but my true love and passion is playing at first base.

"How's it going?" I ask Derek Smyth, one of our starting pitchers as he joins me out on the field.

"Pretty good, how's life treating you?"

"Can't complain," I tell him, not really believing the words that come out of my mouth. I've been in such a funk since returning from the Bahamas. I kick myself in the ass every day for not getting Hannah's information. How I thought just one night with her in my bed was ever going to be enough, I'll never know. The instant way we connected and just clicked isn't something that you can force. It was simply meant to be. I guess if we're meant to meet again, it will happen. I've put that shit out into the universe and hope that it does its magic.

"Kids doing well?" I ask.

"Sure are. They are giving us a run for our money, that's for sure." He laughs. "Being outnumbered sucks sometimes, but that's what happens when we're aiming to have our own baseball team."

"Didn't y'all just have another kid, like, a few months ago?" I ask, hoping I'm keeping everyone's kids in order.

"Yes," he says. "We'd like one, maybe two more, but Jillian also wants to be done with the whole pregnancy stage of life in the next few years. So, I have to go with her desire on that front. As much as I like practicing with my wife and seeing her in all the stages of pregnancy, it is her body after all, and is such an undertaking to bring another human into this world."

"I'll take your word for it," I tell him. While I've been around my friends' girls when they've been pregnant, I've never been right up and in the middle of it. I haven't had someone in my life that a situation like that would be appropriate.

At Derek's mention of his wife growing with their children, my mind immediately flashes to Hannah. I remember the small scar I kissed, and I can't help but wonder what she looks like pregnant. Is she one of those women who is all belly, and you can't even tell they're expecting, or will she be one of those women whose entire body changes?

"Come warm up with me," he says, dragging my attention back to the field in front of us.

We're getting back into the swing of things. Spring training started up this week. It's been a little stressful, but we'll eventually get where we need to be.

I throw the ball back and forth with Derek, with each release of the ball, I can feel my entire body warm up. Today is our first televised pre-season game, not that the starters will play much, as this is the time that all the hopefuls are trying to make the final roster. I remember those days fondly. I spent a couple of years in the minors, one season bouncing back and forth between the AAA affiliate and the big club I was first drafted by before finally securing my full-time starting position, which I held on to for a few seasons before being traded to the Lightning.

There is nothing like the smell of a ball field. The hot dogs and popcorn sometimes waft down to the field, causing my stomach to growl.

Derek and I go through our full warm up cycle, waking up our bodies before it's time for us to return to our locker room for that one last pep talk from Coach, along with the batting order and who he wants out on the field.

With the national anthem over, we take our spots on the field. I'll only be playing the first inning, and then back on the bench I go, for this game.

Once my time on the field is done, I sit back, watching the game unfold in front of me. I can't help but look through the stands at all the people, wishing that I'd one day glance up and find her in the stands. Unfortunately for me, that day isn't today.

SIX

HANNAH

FOUR WEEKS LATER

"Can I get you anything else tonight, Bob?" I ask one of our regular customers. I work a few nights a week as a server. It gets me out of the house and gives me a little bit of income outside of Ryan's life insurance and death benefits. Since he was a financial advisor, he had everything set up that, in the event something ever happened to him, Brayden and I would be taken care of forever. I've been conservative with the money, not wanting to spend it frivolously. He had things set up so our house would be paid off, along with our cars, and the rest would go into savings for us to live off of.

"I'm good, sweetheart, I'll just take the check when you get a moment." I set his bill down on the table, not really sure why he wants one when he orders the exact same thing every time, therefore making his total the exact same each time. He'll leave twenty-five dollars, one crisp twenty and one crisp five-dollar bill. He's done that for the entire time I've worked here and waited on him.

I check in on my other tables, and everyone is content for the time being, so I take a seat for a few minutes. I need to give my poor feet a break.

Courtney's quest into finding Matt has been a big bust. As I figured, the hotel wouldn't release any information due to guest privacy, which I can appreciate. I think the manager she spoke to was understanding why we'd call to ask, but still couldn't help us out.

I head home after my shift. It wasn't super busy tonight, which I was thankful for. I'm going to have to put in my notice sooner than later. My feet are already killing me after my shifts and I'm only a few months pregnant. I haven't really started showing yet, my pants are just now starting to get tight. At home, I usually just live in yoga pants or sweats and baggy shirts, so it is easy to hide. But working requires that I put in a little effort into getting dressed.

"Come sit." Courtney pats the couch once I walk inside my living room. I set my bag and keys down and kick off my shoes before I refill my water bottle in the kitchen and then join her on the couch. "I've got news."

"Did you find him?" I ask, sitting up straighter.

"No, but I did find a PI that thinks he can track down his information," she tells me.

"Really?" I question.

"Yeah, I knew that the other ones we contacted were full of shit," she says.

"How much is that going to cost?" I ask, cringing a little at what she's going to say.

"He has a five-hundred-dollar retainer to start the case. He charges seventy-five an hour and notifies you once he's reached that initial retainer amount. He said that he doesn't think it will cost more than a grand total, but obviously, he doesn't know how quickly he'll get breaks and the information we need."

I blow out a breath and sink back against the couch. I think over my options, is this really what I should do?

"When do we have to get back to him by?" I ask.

"I think anytime. Obviously, the longer we wait, the chances are he takes on other clients and we'd have to wait."

"And you think this is what I should do?" I confirm with Courtney.

"Absolutely. You know you want to find him, and with the limited amount of information you have about him, I really do think this is your only way," she says. "I'm going to really laugh if he was underneath our noses the entire time," she muses.

"Wouldn't that just be hilarious," I say.

"It would. It really would."

We hang out for a little while longer, going over the questionnaire packet the PI sent Courtney. I give him as much information about Matt that I can remember. I include the one picture that I have of him with my son. It isn't much, but maybe he can use that in his search.

"EVENING," I GREET MY NEWEST TABLE. IT'S A four top of twenty-something guys. "Can I get anyone something to drink," I ask, pulling out my pad of paper to write on. I've found, lately, that I have to write down everything. This pregnancy brain is no joke, this time around. I'd forget my own head if it wasn't attached.

Thankfully, this table all orders Cokes, so while they look over the menu, I head for the drink station, filling four glasses with ice and Coke before returning to the table with their drinks.

I pass out the drinks, ready to take their order, when one of them points to one of the many TV screens around the restaurant that play all sorts of sports games. "Looks like Matt O'Riley is next up to bat," one of the guys says. I quickly glance up at the screen and I can't believe who I see, it's *my* Matt. I'm dumbfounded he was right in front of my nose this entire time.

"I'm sorry, what did you say his name was?" I ask the guys.

"That's Matt O'Riley. The first baseman for the Indianapolis Lightning," one of them answers.

"Are you okay?" another asks, placing his hand on

my arm to support me. I guess I started to sway, the shock of seeing Matt on the TV really getting to me.

"Yeah, I'll be fine. Thanks," I say, shaking off the weird feeling I have. "Are you ready to order?" I turn my attention back to the guys.

I get their order in and head for the manager's office. "I'm sorry to do this, but I've got to go. It's an emergency. I just put in an order for table forty-two and they're my only table, at the moment," I tell the manager on duty.

"Is everything okay?" she asks, concern evident in her voice.

"It will be, or at least, I think it will. I just need to get home ASAP." I haven't divulged my pregnancy yet to my work, and now with the revelation that my new baby daddy is none other than a freaking famous base-ball player. It hits me now why Matt was so good with giving Brayden tips for t-ball. It also explains why he was in such good shape.

I run out of the restaurant, not even stopping to text Courtney a heads up that I have news. I speed the entire way back to my house and run inside as soon as I arrive.

"Courtney!" I yell out. "I found him!"

"You what?" she screeches as I come face to face with her in my kitchen. I bend over, needing to suck in a few breaths as I'm winded from running.

"He was on TV at work," I tell her, moving to the living room to find the TV remote. I turn it on, flipping through the channels until I find the baseball game that was on at work.

"Brayden," I call for my son. I want to make sure I'm not just imagining things.

"Yes, Mom," he answers, coming down the hall and into the living room.

"Do you remember the man we met on vacation?" I ask him.

"Mr. Matt?" He gives me a quizzical look.

"Yes, him," I say, crouching down to his level. "Do you remember what he looks like?" I ask, hoping that he'll be shown on the screen sometime soon.

"Yeah," he says, still a little lost to my questioning.

"I think he's a baseball player and I wanted you to tell me if it is him or not," I tell him. The smile that fills his face is promising.

"I knew he played baseball, Mommy. He told me so when we were playing," Brayden tells me. That news knocks me back slightly. Here, my son already had this pertinent information that could have been useful all these weeks, but I never thought to ask him if Matt had told him anything that would help us try and find him.

"He did?" Courtney pipes in, taking a seat on the couch.

"Yep, he plays for the Lightning," Brayden confirms. *Holy shit, I really did find him.* I think to myself.

"There he is, Mommy!" Brayden says, getting all

excited as the camera zooms in on Matt as he adjusts his hat after catching and throwing the ball.

"Damn he's fine," Courtney whispers next to me. "I can see why you'd want to climb him like a tree. You guys are going to have one cute baby."

"Court," I whisper hiss. Brayden still doesn't know that I'm pregnant. I haven't figured out how to tell him yet.

"What," she deadpans, giving me a *tell-me-I'm-wrong* look. "You know I'm right." The smirk she flashes me makes me roll my eyes at her. She might be right about the situation, but that still doesn't mean I can't be annoyed at her.

I'm still so dumbfounded I found him. That I now know his name, know what city and state he lives in. Now, to actually track him down and break the news to him.

"What do I do now?" I ask her.

"First, we cancel the PI. No need for him to do anything else. Apparently, all you had to do was look up at the TV at work." She laughs.

"No shit. It makes me wonder how many other times he'd been on TV, and I never noticed him. Thank God for that table of guys that said something about him, causing me to glance up."

"Right. And hey, it saved you a few hundred bucks."

SEVEN
MATT

I RUN DOWN THE ROAD, SWEAT SOAKING MY TANK top as I close in on mile four of my eight mile run this morning. Spring has sprung here in Indianapolis. The flowers have started to bloom, and the warmer days are sticking around more than not. This is one of my favorite times of the year. It isn't blistering hot out on the field yet, which makes playing outdoors that much more enjoyable.

I slow as I near a park, it is already filling up with families bringing their kids to play on the equipment or for the soccer and t-ball games on the respective fields. Ever since returning from the Bahamas a few months ago, I can't help but scan places kids are, looking for Hannah and Brayden. I kick myself still for not getting her contact information, where they live, or hell, just a last name. I'd do just about anything to go back in time to that night and ask more questions. But I can't, so I'm the creep that scopes out all the kids and moms at the park when I run by. I know the likelihood I'll ever find them again would be like finding a needle in a haystack, but a man can dream.

I pick back up once I'm past the park. I need to get back home so I can shower and head over to Justin's place. He's having most of us over for a get together. We've got a random weekend off early in the season, so we're taking full advantage.

"Hey, Matt," JJ's wife, Riley, greets when I walk through their back gate. She's got their son, Easton, on her hip.

"Hey, Riley, how are you doing today?" I ask her, running a hand over the top of Easton's head.

"Great, thanks for asking. How's the start of the season going for you?" she asks.

"Can't complain. I think we're off to a good start so far. Hopefully, we can repeat like last year."

"Wouldn't that be nice!" she says. "The guys are all on the patio if you want to go find them."

"Thanks," I say before heading around the corner and to the patio area. Sure enough, I find a handful of my teammates, their wives or girlfriends, and a sea of kids all running around and playing. Some jumping into the pool, others playing tag or some other kid game out in the grass.

"Matt!" JJ's booming voice calls out over the noise of the crowd. "About time you made it," he teases as I reach where he's standing. I exchange bro-hugs with all the guys, leaning down to give Derek's wife, Jillian, a kiss on her cheek, as well as Carmen, our PR manager, and Lucas Black's fiancée.

"Sorry I'm late, went out for an eight-mile run this morning," I tell everyone.

"What didn't you understand about a day off?" Lucas teases.

"Can't get lazy," I tell him. "Plus, I never feel like I accomplished anything if I don't get in some form of exercise every day."

"Whatever you say, man." Lucas smacks me on the back.

"What's going on around here? Did I miss anything important?"

"Just shooting the sh-crap," Derek says, correcting himself from cussing around all the kids.

"I heard that," his wife, Jillian, pipes in.

"Hey, I caught myself." He laughs.

"Matt, I have a question for you," Carmen says.

"I'll do my best to answer," I tell her, swinging my attention in her direction.

"Do you like dogs?" she asks, and I wasn't expecting a question like that. I was ready to be hit with the "are you single" question.

"Sure," I answer honestly. Since I'm single, and with my travel schedule, I've never considered getting a pet, as it wouldn't be fair to them to be alone or boarded all the time.

"A local pet rescue sent a request asking if any of our players would be willing to participate in a charity calendar. You'd be posed with some of their available dogs, then they'll compile the pictures, make the calendar and sell them to help support their organization."

"I could do that," I tell her.

"I'd be down for that if they need more of us," Derek offers.

"Same, I think we'd all be willing to help," JJ tells her.

"Awesome! Thanks, guys. I'll email the lady and let her know. They set everything up. So once I've had the chance to go over the schedule with her and find a time for all of you to shoot, I'll let y'all know," Carmen informs us.

We shoot the shit for the rest of the day, grill out for lunch and dinner, and just enjoy the much-needed day off. A baseball season is long and can be tiring, so taking advantage of time off is important.

I walk out of the dugout, my glove under my arm as I open a bottle of water and take a long pull from it. The sun is already out in full force, it's going to be a hot one today. The fans are already starting to slowly file in as the gates opened not that long ago. Most of the players arrived hours ago, me included. We all have our own game-day routines, but for most of the guys, they're here hours early. I, personally, start out with a light workout, some time with the athletic trainers to get fully stretched out, then some time in the ice bath, if needed, for some muscle recovery. We usually have some time to watch tape on the other team, followed by a meal, and finally it's warm-up time before the game starts.

It's all a production, a lifestyle that most players live by.

I scan over the fans milling around, some coming down as close to the field as they can to snap pictures as the players all start to funnel out to warm up. I've taken to scanning every face I can, hoping for fate to be on my side and for Hannah and Brayden to magically appear one day. I do a double take when I see a woman with chestnut hair, pulled back into a ponytail, with a boy, but upon looking closer, I see that it isn't them.

I slide my sunglasses over my eyes, toss the now empty water bottle into the trash can, and pick up a baseball from the ground. It's time to focus and get into game mode.

I toss the ball into the air, catching it as it comes down perfectly into my glove. I repeat this motion fifteen times. Always the same number of times, always have, and always will. Many players have superstitions, and this right here is mine.

I scan the field, searching to see who else has come out to warm up. JJ and Derek are warming up as Derek is our starting pitcher today. I catch Lucas' eye, throwing the ball in my hand his direction. He snags the ball like the expert he is, right out of the air, sending it back my way just as fast.

Once our arms are warmed up, I take some practice swings, making sure I'll be ready when it's my time to be up to bat. Superstition number two comes into play when I'm standing at home plate. Three taps of my bat on the plate, hands stacked on the bat as it taps my shoulder, before hovering just above it as I wait on the pitcher to send the ball my way. Much like throwing the ball into the air and catching it fifteen times in a row being something I've always done, I've always done this when it's my time to bat. I've perfected both over the years, but the basics are the same.

"Matt, can we get your autograph?" I hear a kid call out. I survey the crowd and see a young boy holding out a sharpie. I have a hard time telling kids no, so when I'm done warming up, I jog over to the sidelines and sign the kid's jersey. "Thank you so much, Mr. O'Riley," the boy thanks me.

"Anytime, thanks for being a fan," I tell him as his mom holds her phone up to snag a picture of the two of us. I sign a few more things for others who have crowded around. Security starts to close in, and that's my sign I've got to clear out.

It's the bottom of the ninth, we're tied at five, and we've got the bases loaded when I'm up to bat. All it would take is a fly ball to the outfield to get JJ home and for this game to be over.

I stare the pitcher down, watching for his ticks that he so desperately tries to hide, but I've picked up on. I can usually determine what kind of pitch he's sending my way, giving me the opportunity to make any minor adjustment I need.

The first ball he throws is a fastball. Unfortunately for him, it's a ball and not an out. I step back as he works out with his catcher what he's sending my way for this second pitch. I step back up, tap my bat on the plate, tap my shoulder, and wait. His second pitch is a curveball, I swing but foul the ball out.

Two more pitches are sent my way, another foul, another ball. The fifth pitch he throws my way connects and I know right away this is it. The crack of the bat hitting the ball is perfection. I don't need to wait on the announcer, I know this ball is out of here. A walk-off mother-fucking grand slam to win the game.

I run the bases, my smile bright as I round third base and head home. My entire team is waiting for me at home plate to celebrate the win. I'm doused in water, the ice a shock to my body.

"That's how we fucking do it!" someone shouts out as I attempt to wipe water and sweat from my eyes.

The crowd is still going crazy as we disperse. What an amazing game we just gave them tonight. I can't wait to see the replays that will come from tonight's game. That grand slam should be headline news on SportsCenter later.

I'm stopped by our PR department, I'm the lucky one they want to interview for the fans, both in the stadium and those either listening on the radio or watching at home.

"Matt, can you walk us through that last at bat?"

"Yeah, it was pretty fun, I'd say," I laugh. "I just waited the pitcher out, when that final pitch came my way, I knew that it was the perfect one. The moment that ball hit my bat, I knew it was going to be the end of things. I believed that we could pull off this win, and we showed up tonight and pulled off the W," I say into the microphone.

The fans apparently like my answer as they start to chant my name. I hold up a hand, thanking them for the enthusiasm. This is one of the reasons players do what we do. The love we have for this game is tenfold when the fans are just as into it as we are.

I answer a few more questions before the interview ends, and I head into the dugout and down into the locker room. I'm greeted once again by my rowdy teammates.

After that game, I'm feeling pretty damn good. I strip out of my uniform, wrap a towel around my waist, and head for the showers. The hot water on my muscles feels amazing. I'm sure I'll be sore come tomorrow morning. I'll have to come in early to get in with one of the team massage therapists.

I take the longest shower known to man, letting the water run until I'm all out of hot water. By the time I make my way back to my locker, most of the guys have already cleared out, heading home to their families or out to celebrate at some bar.

I get dressed in some jeans and a T-shirt. Nothing fancy, as I just plan to stop for some takeout and to head home.

As I exit the locker room, one of the security guards who's been with this team longer than I have calls my name.

"What's up, Charles?" I ask. I accept his handshake, pulling him in for a man hug.

"There's a young boy out there asking for you. I told him I'd see what I could do about getting you back out on the field."

"They're still here?" I ask, checking my watch.

"Yep, I was just talking to them before I heard the door open."

"Thanks, man." I give him a fist bump before clearing the two steps up into the dugout and onto the field.

I look to both sides of the dugout as Charles didn't say exactly where they were waiting.

"Matt!" I hear my name being called and the voice has me snapping my head to the left. *Brayden?*

I take a triple take, not believing whom I'm seeing standing there by the railings that separates the stands from the field. I close the distance in a matter of seconds.

"Brayden!" I say his name, it comes out almost as a whisper due to my shock of them being here.

"I told you, Mommy," I hear him saying to Hannah. I roam my eyes over her, and fuck she takes my breath away. They've both got on Lightning shirts, and Brayden is sporting a baseball hat, as well, with the logo front and center.

"Hannah," I say her name in greeting.

"Hi, Matt," she says, waiting shyly. "I hope you don't mind that we asked if you were available."

"Absolutely not. Do you want to come down here?" I ask. "I could give you a quick tour of the behind-the-scenes areas."

"Can we, Mommy?" Brayden asks, jumping up and down.

"I guess so," she agrees. I point to an area that has a gate and walk along as they make their way to it. I open the latch, watching as Brayden hops down the steps. I hold out a hand for Hannah to take, making sure she doesn't fall as she takes the steps. Most of the flood-lights have been shut off already, so it isn't as bright as it was during the game. The moment her hand touches mine, a spark shoots up my arm and into my body. My dick swells at the memories of the last time we were together.

"Do you live here?" I ask, still dumbfounded they are actually standing in front of me. "In Indianapolis, I mean," I add on to my question.

Hannah lets go of my hand, her hand going to Brayden's shoulder as we stand facing one another. "No," she says, shaking her head before her eyes drop down to Brayden. "We live in Springfield, Illinois, but came here to see you," she says, a little nervously.

"I'm glad that you did. I've hated myself for not getting your number before we parted ways," I tell her honestly, and her eyes fly to mine.

"You what?" she asks, blinking fast as if that will help her process what I've just said easier.

"I've tried everything I can think of besides hiring a private investigator to try and find you," I admit.

"Oh my god," she whispers, bringing her hand to cover her mouth. "I'd almost hired one to find you," she says. "But you saved the day when your smiling face showed up on the TV and I finally learned your last name and where I could find you. Little did I know that Brayden, here, knew who you were all along."

"Now that is kind of hilarious." I chuckle. "How long are the two of you in town for?" I ask, not wanting to let them go, but also realizing that it is late, and I know Brayden needs to get to bed soon.

"A few days. We drove over, so we're flexible," she says.

"How about we table the tour until tomorrow, when the facility isn't trying to close down. More of the guys will be around that I can introduce you to, as well. How does that sound, Brayden?" I ask him, dropping to his level.

"Can we, Mom, please?" he asks, turning her direction and flashing some damn good puppy-dog eyes.

"I don't know how you can say no to that face," I muse.

"You get used to it after a while. But I think tabling the tour until tomorrow is a great idea. It's so late, we need to get back to the Airbnb so I can get someone off to bed."

"Can I get your number, first, then I'll text you mine and we can get in touch tomorrow and set something up."

"That's perfect," Hannah says. I pull out my cell, opening the contacts app, tapping the option to create a new entry. I add her first name, then just hand the phone over to her to add her information. She hands it back and I select the option to send her a message. I text a quick *hello, this is Matt,* to her phone, hearing it ping seconds after I hit send on my end.

"Did you drive to the stadium?" I ask as I start leading them out.

"No, we Ubered it here. I didn't want to deal with the parking."

"I can drive you back," I offer right away.

"Are you sure, we don't want to interrupt your evening," she says.

"All I was going to do was grab some food and head home. Are you hungry?"

"No, we're good. Ate way too much stadium food tonight." She laughs, and the sound takes me back to the beach and those few magical days we spent together. "If you're positive it isn't an imposition, we won't turn down a ride home. I was just going to Uber it back. If it is more convenient to stop and get food, first, please do so."

"I'm easy," I tell her. "How far away are you?"

"Not super far, maybe ten blocks or so. Far enough that I knew it would be too far of a walk, but close enough that an Uber wasn't going to be super expensive."

"No problem at all," I tell her as I lead them out to the players' lot. My car is the last one here, as everyone cleared out long ago.

I hit the unlock button as we approach, opening the side doors. I hold them open as Brayden and Hannah get settled, closing them once I know they're secured in.

I quickly round the car, getting into the driver's seat and starting the car. "What's the address?" I ask, tapping on the screen to pull up my GPS. I enter the address she gives me before pulling out of my parking spot. I want so desperately to reach over and grab her hand, or to place my hand on her thigh. Having her so close to me, in my space, yet not being able to touch her any way I want is taking all of my control.

I SUCK IN A DEEP BREATH. I CAN'T BELIEVE I found him. Then had the nerve to actually make a trip to find him and am now sitting in his car.

I try hard not to stare at him, but I can't help it. I've seen this man completely naked, had him inside me in the most intimate of ways, but I still find myself nervous. Nervous how he'll take the news I have to give him. Nervous what that means for life moving forward. Will he get mad and never want to see us again? Will he embrace the unknown and want to be in his child's life -- in my and Brayden's lives? I have to have a shred of hope that it is the latter, but you never really know how someone is going to react to this type of situation until they're actually confronted with it.

"Are you sure you don't mind if I stop to grab something to eat quick?" he asks as we pull out of the parking lot.

"Not at all," I tell him. "Thanks again for the ride." I glance back at Brayden. I can tell he's fading fast, now that he's sat still for more than thirty seconds. Add in that it is pitch black outside and well past his bedtime, he's going to crash as soon as his head hits the pillow.

"I'll just grab something from a drive-through so it's quick."

"Are you sure? I didn't think athletes eat that kind of food."

"I don't make a habit of it, but one meal isn't going to hurt."

"How long have you been playing?" I ask, just wanting to fill the time.

"So, you haven't Googled me?" He smirks.

"Maybe just a little," I confess, and I can feel my cheeks heating. Thank God it is dark in the car, and he can't see them.

"I've played since I was about Brayden's age. My love for the game started young. I made my way up from t-ball to little league, which morphed into travel ball, followed by high school and two seasons in college before I went pro."

"And how long have you been here in Indianapolis?" I ask.

"This is my sixth season with the Lightning. I was drafted by the Giants, played a few seasons with them before being traded."

"How much longer can you play for?"

He chuckles. "Every athlete would love to know

that answer, but unfortunately, that is a huge unknown. I could get injured tomorrow and be done, or I could go on to play multiple more seasons. There are a ton of variables when it comes to an athlete's career."

"Makes sense." I nod my head in agreement. "I'll rephrase, how much longer do you hope to play?"

"Two, maybe three more seasons. I'm getting up there in age. The toll the job takes on my body isn't getting any easier, nor is the travel. The baseball season is long, with a lot of games packed into it."

"We've watched a few of your games," I admit. "Brayden gets so excited when they show you on TV."

"I've scanned every crowd this season, hoping that I might spot the two of you," he admits, turning to make eye contact with me for a brief second.

"You have?!" I gasp at his admission.

"Yes," he answers. "The only regret I have from our time together back in December was not getting your number, so walking out to find the two of you tonight was the best surprise ever."

We pause our conversation long enough for him to order and get his food. The butterflies in my stomach take flight at his admission. The fact that this man has been missing us, and possibly looking for us, just like I was of him is reassuring and makes me believe that he won't run when I drop my news in his lap. I still don't know when or how I'm going to tell him, but now that I have him here, I need to figure that part out ASAP.

Matt pulls into the driveway, killing the engine as I turn to find Brayden passed out in the back seat. "He had such a long day," I murmur.

"Let me carry him inside for you," Matt offers.

I don't even fight him. I get out and open the passenger door so I can reach in and get Brayden unbuckled. Once he's ready, I step out of the way, brushing against Matt's hard body, the feel instantly bringing back so many amazing memories from our night together.

He slides a hand across my back, pausing for a couple seconds as he grips my hip, steadying me. "Careful now, I don't need you tripping and hurting yourself. I can only carry one of you at a time." He smirks and turns to get Brayden out of the car. I don't know how he does this so gracefully, but he does. With my sleeping son on his shoulder, I lead him to the front door and inside the rental. I turn on a lamp, allowing for some light so we don't trip on anything as we make our way to one of the bedrooms. I pull the blankets back and step aside so he can place Brayden in the bed. Once he's down, I slip his shoes and socks off, then tuck him in. I don't have the energy to attempt to change him out of his T-shirt and shorts tonight.

I head back out to the living room and find Matt sitting at the little table, eating his sandwich and fries. "Want some?" he offers, holding up the container of fries. The smell of them is tempting, but I already had so much greasy, not-that-healthy food today.

"I'm good," I tell him. Instead of the mouth-watering fries, I grab a banana off the counter, peeling it as I take a seat across from him.

Now that it is just the two of us, I have no idea what to say to this man. The silence between us feels charged and like you could cut it with a knife. We stare one another down, waiting to see who will crack first.

Matt smirks before placing the last bite of his sandwich in his mouth. I can't help but watch as he licks the sauce from his fingers, wishing his tongue was licking my nipples, or better yet, my clit.

"I could tell you what I believe you're thinking right now." His sexy, raspy voice fills the room and snaps me from my delirium.

I'm like a fish out of water, my mouth opening and closing as I attempt to find words. Words that won't give away the X-rated things that were just running through my mind moments before. Thoughts that usually aren't far from my mind when Matt is on my brain.

"And what might that be?" I finally spit out, my cheeks definitely on fire now.

He leans forward, running a finger down my cheek before he cups my face and runs the pad of his thumb over my lips. He pushes it inside and I instantly suck on the tip of it, flicking my tongue over the pad.

"Fuck," he curses, standing so quickly, the chair he's sitting in scrapes along the wood floor and crashes back, falling over. He pulls me up and out of my chair, bringing us chest-to-chest. "I've wanted to kiss you for so damn long, tell me to stop if you don't want the same, Hannah."

I stay quiet as I stare up at him. His eyes are hooded with desire. Desire for *me*. I find an ounce of courage and push up on my toes, all while bringing a hand to the back of his neck so I can pull him down to me. Our lips meet gently, but only for the briefest of moments. His control snaps as the desperation takes over as we both explore.

I've only just recently started to show, and that is only to those that know me and see me on a regular basis. At this point, it still just looks like I'm rocking a food baby, so I'm not worried that my current knocked-up status will be a dead giveaway before I can actually tell Matt the news.

All thoughts of my pregnant status fall to the wayside when he slips his hands under my T-shirt and up my torso until he reaches my bra. My breasts have been so sensitive this go around. I shudder when he cups them, flicking my nipples.

"Are you okay?" He immediately stops kissing me and touching my nipples to ask.

"I'll be fine, just extra sensitive," I tell him honestly. I know I need to tell him, and should before anything else happens between us, so I guess this is my chance.

I link our hands together, leading him to the couch. We take a seat and I turn to face him.

"Is everything okay?" he asks, tucking a chunk of hair behind my ear.

"Um," I say, not sure if I should just blurt it out or work up to telling him. Why don't these types of situations come with an instruction manual. "I-I'm..." *Fuck, I'm going to be sick.* I jump off the couch and cover my mouth as I run for the bathroom.

Once I empty the contents of my stomach into the toilet, I splash a little water on my face and quickly rinse my mouth out before brushing my teeth. "Hannah, are you okay?" Matt asks from the other side of the closed door.

I open it and look at him. Tears burn my eyes as I find an ounce of courage and the words. "I'm pregnant." There, I said it, I got the words out.

He continues to watch me and I'm not sure my words have sunk in. Not that I've explained everything.

"Okay," he says. "Is everything okay with you and the baby?" he asks, pulling me into his arms.

I swipe at the tears that are running down my cheeks before I rest my head against his chest. The sound of his heartbeat calming in the best ways possible.

"Yeah," I tell him. "Matt, the baby is yours," I whisper, needing him to know, yet praying at the same time that he doesn't push me away.

"Fuck yes, it is," he says, dropping a kiss to the top of my head.

I bark out a half cry-half laugh strangled noise as I

lean back so I can look up at him in amazement. This is the best response I could have dreamed of getting, but it still shocks me.

"You're not mad?" I ask.

"Hell no. This isn't your fault, just as much as it isn't mine. We took every precaution we could that night, but obviously the universe has other ideas. Ones that we didn't yet know that we needed."

I'm astonished by this man. Who is he and where did he come from?

"I had no idea how I was going to find you, but I was doing everything I could to do so. I tried to get the resort to give me your contact information, but they wouldn't due to privacy reasons. I even asked the lady if she'd contact you and give you my information so you could call me, but they still wouldn't do that."

"Damn," he says, shaking his head.

"Then, one day your face was plastered on the TVs at work, and I about fell over."

"I guess it's a good thing the cameras love me." He smirks. "And I'm glad that you came here to tell me. I want to be in your lives. I want this baby to know that he or she has a mom and dad that loves them," he says as he places a hand against my abdomen. I can't stop the tears from falling. *Damn pregnancy hormones.*

"I was so worried you'd hate me. Accuse me of trying to trap you, or worse, say you wanted nothing to do with us and send me on my way." I spill all my fears out at his feet. "But I also had immense hope that you wouldn't respond that way. That you'd be the sweet man I met on the beach a few months ago. The one that took time out of his day to play catch with my son, and the one that thought of him just as much as you thought of me before our date."

"I'm glad that you had good thoughts about me. I won't lie and say I'm perfect, but I don't back down from my responsibilities, either. What can I do to help? I don't want to overstep, but I want to be there as much as I can. My schedule, especially until the end of the season -- and lord willing, the end of the post season, will be hectic, but I'll be there as much as I can. I want to experience everything I can."

"I don't really need anything right now. I've had two appointments with my OB/GYN, and everything has been perfect so far. They did a dating ultrasound at my first one to give me a due date, and at the second appointment it was just the normal pee in a cup, take some blood, ask, and answer questions. Since this isn't my first pregnancy, I didn't have many."

"Okay, well, if you think of something, you'll let me know?" he asks.

"Yes," I agree quickly.

"When is your next appointment?" he asks.

"In a few weeks, I just went last Friday. I'm still early enough that I only go once a month."

"Can you send me the date and time? If I can make it work, I'd like to come, if you're okay with that."

I'm a little shocked he's so open to this so quickly, but also so happy that he is.

"Of course," I tell him, stepping out of his embrace to find my cell. I pull up my calendar app so I can give him the info.

"We get back from a road trip the night before, and that just so happens to be an off day, so I'll be there," he says. "I'll have to head back that night because we have practice the next day, but I'll at least be able to come for the appointment and be there for the day."

"Sounds like a plan, and if I need to move the appointment, I can do so. They're pretty flexible."

"No, that one will work. Do you have more scheduled?"

"Nope, I just book one at a time. So, I'll make my next one at that one and so on."

"Do you get to have another ultrasound anytime soon?" he asks.

"They typically do the *big*," I use air quotes to emphasize the word big, "ultrasound, where most people find out the gender, at twenty weeks. There is an ultrasound and blood test offered around fourteen weeks to rule out things like Down syndrome or Trisomy 18, but I declined it. My anatomy scan is at my next appointment, so you'll be able to be there for that."

"Wow!" he says, a little shocked. "How far along are you and when is the baby due?"

"Sixteen weeks and I'm due mid-September," I tell him.

"Shit, that's smack dab in the middle of playoffs. I'll warn you now that I might miss the birth, and I'm sorry for that."

"We'll figure it all out when the time comes," I assure him.

He cups my face and closes the small amount of distance between us. "Thank you for finding me and telling me." He brings his forehead to mine as he holds me tight. "I don't know what the future holds for us, but I'd like to do our due diligence and get to know each other, and if you're ready for a relationship, maybe give this a try."

I'm already floating on cloud nine after his near-perfect reaction to the news, but to now hear that he wants me -- us, and potentially as more than just a co-parenting relationship has new tears falling from my eyes.

NINE
MATT

I wipe the tears from Hannah's face, still a little shocked she's here in front of me. The fact that I'm going to be a dad hits me hard. I already feel like I've missed so much in the months since we were last together. It also isn't lost on me that we were both looking for each other. Fate is funny that way, sometimes. Brings people together when you least expect it to happen.

"Don't cry, sweetheart," I murmur, my lips pressed against her skin. "Everything will work out the way it's supposed to," I say as her body shakes with her cries. I can only imagine the worry and emotional roller coaster she's gone through since finding out she was pregnant. From the emotional standpoint of being a single mom already, to the fact that we didn't really know one another. Add in the stress of trying to find me, and I can understand why she's falling apart in my arms.

I hold her as tight as I can, wanting to shoulder any of her stress. Once her cries slow, and her body stops trembling, I scoop her up in my arms, carrying her to the bedroom opposite from where Brayden sleeps. I set her on the end of the bed, then duck into the bathroom. There isn't a tub, so a hot shower will have to do. I turn the water on, making sure it will get nice and hot in here. I rummage around in the basket of amenities on the counter, finding a shower steamer tablet, and I toss it in so it can start to dissolve.

"Come here and strip," I say, standing in the doorway. I've already unbuckled my belt and the top button of my jeans. My T-shirt is untucked and ready to be pulled off.

"What-why?" she questions, a confused but cute expression on her face.

"You need to relax, so we're going to take a hot shower. I'm going to do all the work and then tuck you into bed once you're all relaxed," I tell her.

She must think my idea is a good one as she stands from the edge of the bed where I'd left her and pulls her shirt over her head. Her breasts almost spill over the tops of the cups and I can tell they've gotten fuller than the last time I saw them.

Once she lowers her pants, I can't miss the slight swell of her abdomen. It wasn't noticeable in the clothes she was wearing, but it is now. That's my baby.

Our baby. The one I already love more than I can even describe.

Hannah slowly walks towards me in nothing but her bra and panties. My dick swells and presses against the confines of my briefs and pants. I can't get enough of this woman, and I've hardly touched her tonight.

She stops in front of me, seeing as how I'm blocking her way into the bathroom. Hannah glances up at me, her eyes now displaying a look of desire and hope. "We take this one hour, one day, one moment at a time," I say as I pull her into my arms. I have the ultimate desire to claim her, to make her mine in every way possible. I drop my lips to hers, capturing her lips as a starting point.

She slides her hands under my shirt, the feeling of her skin against my own sending tingles down my body as my cock swells even more.

"I think you're a little overdressed," she says, breaking the kiss. I reach behind my head, grabbing my T-shirt and pulling it off in one swift move. I quickly follow that up by unzipping my jeans and shoving them down my body, taking my briefs with them. Once off my ankles, I kick everything out of the way. I don't need her tripping on something.

I palm my cock, giving it a few strokes as I watch Hannah as she watches me. "Now who's overdressed?" I ask, seeing as I'm now naked and she's still got on panties and her bra.

She smirks and reaches behind her back,

unclasping her bra. The straps fall from her shoulders before the cups follow suit. I can't help it, I've got to touch her, so I reach up and cup her full breasts in my hands. She sucks in a breath and I'm careful, seeing as how sensitive she is right now. While I cup her breasts, she shimmies out of her panties and my desire for this woman shoots through the roof.

I rein in my desires and lead her into the water. I'm not here to just fuck her and leave her. No, I'm here to show her how much I want her. How much I want something to spark and grow between us other than the baby she's already growing.

"Oh my god," she moans once under the hot spray.

"Feel good?" I ask, rubbing her shoulders as I stand behind her. My cock throbbing as her ass nestles against it.

"So good," she confirms, her head rolling forward as she relaxes into the water and my touch. I continue to knead the knots in her muscles; the more the water warms her, the more she relaxes and the tension melts away under my touch. The water cools slightly, so I reach behind me and turn it up again. I hope this place has a large hot water tank as I plan to be in here for as long as we possibly can.

I work my way down her back, kneading the muscles as I go. Once I reach her hips, I stop my massage and move to wash her hair. I love the way she's allowed me to take over, putting her pleasure into my hands.

Once she's washed and relaxed, I turn the water off and step out of the shower, grabbing one of the large fluffy towels on the rack. I wrap her up, making sure she's good before I grab a towel for myself. I dry off quickly, then wrap the towel around my hips, tucking the end in to hold it in place.

"Do you need anything before bed?" I ask.

"Just to do my bathroom stuff," she answers, and I step out of the room so she can do so in private.

While she's in the bathroom, I gather my clothes, slipping back into my underwear and jeans. I leave them undone, not sure what's going to happen tonight. I don't want to pressure Hannah. I'm not sure if she's comfortable with me staying here tonight or not. That might be a bit quick and something she's not ready to discuss with Brayden.

The door opens and she walks out, her hair no longer wrapped in a towel. It is now brushed, but still wet and hanging down to her shoulders. Her face is cleaned from the small amount of makeup and is glowing. She could go without a stitch of any and still look gorgeous. She's pulled on an oversized T-shirt that I didn't realize she'd grabbed at some point.

"I wasn't sure if you were comfortable with me staying the night or if I should go. I'll do whatever you want," I tell her, hoping that she hears the sincerity in my voice.

"Oh, yeah. It would probably be best if you weren't here in the morning. I'm not ready for

Brayden to wake up to me in bed with a man," she says quietly.

"I completely understand," I tell her as I stand and finish getting dressed. "Why don't you walk me out so you can lock up behind me and then call me in the morning once you guys are up and moving around. I've got practice for a few hours, but otherwise, I'm free the rest of the day and evening. If you want to bring him over to the stadium for practice, I can arrange for you to be let in."

"He'd love that, and then we could take that tour you promised him."

"Exactly." I smile down at her. As much as I'd love to have this woman in my arms tonight, I know that I can't rush this. She's in my life for the foreseeable future, I can only hope it's in a bigger way than just my child's mother.

TEN
HANNAH

"Hey, buddy, how'd you sleep?" I ask Brayden as he comes out of the bedroom, still a little sleepy-eyed.

"Good." He yawns and wraps his favorite blanket around his body before plopping down on the couch. He turns on some cartoon while he relaxes and wakes up.

"Are you hungry for some breakfast?" I ask. "Matt said we can come over to the stadium to watch them practice, and then get a tour if you still want to do that."

"Can we go now?" he asks, popping up with excitement.

I can't help but laugh at how quickly he went from being half asleep still to being wide awake and ready to run out the door. "Not yet, buddy. I don't think practice starts for a few more hours." I realize I have no idea what time we should head over, Matt never told me last night.

Hannah: Good morning, I hope I'm not waking you. I was just wondering what time we should plan on showing up at the stadium. I realize you never said a time last night.

Matt: Oh, sorry about that. Official practice starts at ten and goes until noon.

Hannah: As opposed to unofficial practice?

Matt: A lot of the guys show up before that to see the trainers or massage therapists, or even come in early to hit the weight room.

Hannah: Oh, that makes sense. So, should we plan to arrive around ten, then? How will we get in? Or is it open to the public?

Matt: It isn't open to the public. I'm headed in there shortly; I'm going to stop into the office and find out how to get the two of you in and I'll let you know.

Hannah: That works!

Matt: We can go grab some lunch afterward, sound good?

Hannah: Sounds like a plan.

Matt: Do the two of you like tacos? There's a local Mexican restaurant where a lot of us on the team goes. It's quiet and we don't get bothered there.

Hannah: Brayden and I love tacos, so that sounds good to me.

Matt: It's a date then.

I set my phone aside. My stomach is starting to growl. I need to get some food in me, especially since I lost my stomach contents last night.

"What would you like for breakfast?" I ask Brayden.

"Cereal," he says, his attention having been sucked back in by the show he's watching.

I've been soaking up these months with him. His birthday was very close to the cut-off for starting kindergarten last fall, but I just felt like he'd be better off being red-shirted and waiting one more year to start.

I pull out a bowl and fill it with some cereal and milk. "Come to the table, please, your breakfast is ready."

I pull out a bagel, dropping it into the toaster while I pull the cream cheese out of the fridge.

"Matt said after he's done with practice, he'll give us the tour and then we get to go to lunch. He wants to take us to his favorite taco place," I explain to Brayden.

"Okay. Can I get a ball when we're at the stadium?"

"I'm sure you can. You might even get some of the guys to sign it for you. Matt did say something last night about you getting to meet some of his teammates."

"That will be so cool, Mom. Everyone back home will think it's cool."

"I'm sure they will," I agree with him as I spread cream cheese on my bagel. I pour myself a cup of coffee and sit down to have some breakfast with my son.

Matt

I KNOCK ON THE DOORFRAME, WAITING FOR Carmen to acknowledge me before I walk in the open door.

"Matt, how are you today?" Carmen greets.

I slide a hand along the back of my neck, squeezing it to relieve some of the tension that has built up overnight. I slept like shit last night, if I'm being honest—more like lain in my bed wide awake, staring at the ceiling as so many things ran through my mind. "Um," I stammer, trying to find the words I need.

I close her door, not wanting what I'm about to disclose to become office gossip. "I might have a situation on my hands and need some advice and maybe some help," I tell her. I know Carmen is one of the best in the PR world, hell, she'd have to be to put up with dating Lucas.

"Okay, this must be serious if I know nothing

already and you'd shut my door. Sit and spill," she instructs.

I take a seat in one of the chairs across from her, ready to spill my guts about what's happened since the game ended last night.

"Do you remember that woman I met when we went to the Caribbean?"

"The single mom who you had the hot little fling with?" she asks, her curiosity obvious.

"Yeah," I admit, not realizing that anyone knew about the fling part. "I've spent the last few months looking for her. We had this instant connection, but like the dumbass I am, we only exchanged first names. I didn't ask where she was from or lived. All I knew about her was her name was Hannah and she was a widowed mother to a five-year-old. I was considering hiring a PI to track her down, but never did."

"Okay, so what do you need my help with? Tracking her down?" she asks, already jotting some things down on a notepad.

"No," I say, a smile already filling my face. "She tracked me down and showed up at yesterday's game. Her and Brayden, that's her son, stayed after the game and flagged down one of the security guards and asked if he could send me out. You know I have a hard time saying no to a kid who wants an autograph."

"Aww, now if that isn't the sweetest thing I've ever heard, I don't know what is," she says, practically swooning in her seat.

"There's more," I tell her. "Even with all precautions taken on our one night together, we're having a baby."

"Wow, okay. We can handle this," she says, jotting down a few more things.

"I've already told her I want to be involved as much as possible. The distance is going to be a pain in my ass, but we'll figure it out," I tell Carmen.

"Where does she live?" she asks.

"Springfield, so not super far, but not here in Indy, either."

"At least it is only one state over. She could be across the country."

"I know. I'm going to head there in a few weeks for her next doctor's appointment. I guess it is the one when they do the big ultrasound. I've already checked the schedule and it just so happens to be on an off day right after we get back from a road trip."

"Okay. So how public do you want to be with this?" Carmen asks. I hadn't really thought about that. I was coming to Carmen more as a friend, not a PR person. "We can release a statement or stay mum about everything. It's up to you. Eventually, the press is going to get wind of things; we can't keep it hidden forever."

"I have no idea; can I get back to you on that after I discuss it with Hannah?" I ask.

"Of course, and if you want me to talk to her, I'd be happy to do so."

"The main reason I came to you today is for some

help. I promised Brayden a tour and need help getting them into the stadium to watch practice. Can you meet them outside and let them in?"

"Absolutely! Just text her my number and have her call me when they arrive, and I'll run down and let them in."

"Thanks, Carmen. And can you keep them just between us, for now? I'd like to tell the guys on my own terms."

"My lips are sealed. That even goes for Lucas," she says. I know she'd never break someone's trust by spilling our personal news to anyone, and that includes her boyfriend who is one of my teammates and good friends.

"Thanks," I tell her as I shoot a text off to Hannah with Carmen's information and instructions to call or text her to get into the stadium for practice.

"You probably won't have much time to tell them, they're going to be quite interested in your visitors," she warns before I open her door.

"I'm aware," I tell her, already wondering what the reaction in the locker room will be.

I head first for Coach's office. I figure it is professional of me to tell him what's going on in my personal life as it may get out in the press and cause some unwanted stress.

He's a levelheaded and straightforward guy. Takes the news like I figured he would. Congratulated me on my pending fatherhood, but also advised I need to keep my head in the game and focused on my job. Some might find that kind of advice dick-ish, but I get where he's coming from. It is his job to keep this team on track and focused on winning.

"Ready to hit the weights?" JJ asks from his perch in front of his locker as he finishes tying his laces.

"Give me a few, just need to get changed," I tell him as I strip from my street clothes.

"Where have you been hiding today? Your car was already in the lot when I got here. I figured you'd already be in the weight room," he says as he waits for me to change.

"Needed to talk to Carmen and Coach," I tell him. If anyone in this locker room knows what it's like to have a surprise baby, it is JJ. His situation was much different, seeing as how his baby mama dropped his daughter off on his doorstep and hasn't been involved since. Signed her rights away and everything. Thankfully, Derek's little sister Riley had just moved to town and stepped in to be his nanny and, well, now they're married and have a baby on the way.

"What scandal have you found yourself in?" he asks.

I bark out a laugh. "Why does it have to be a scandal?" I ask. "I'm not the bad-boy of baseball like you used to be."

"PR and the coaching staff. That usually has scandal written all over it," he says, shrugging his shoulders.

I finish tying my own shoes, jumping up to my feet, ready to head for the weight room and sweat like crazy.

"You know how I've kind of been broody since returning from the beach in December?" I ask.

"Yeah," he says.

"I'd met someone there. Fast forward to last night, she tracked me down and showed up here after the game. I took her back to her place last night," I say, and he interrupts me.

"Hell yeah, you did. About time you got laid."

"Shut the fuck up," I tell him. "That's not what happened. At all," I say. "She's got a little boy, Brayden. He's five and quite the kid. I met him at the beach, as well. Anyway, I drove them back to their Airbnb and we talked. She's having my baby," I tell him, getting it out before I chicken out.

JJ stops in his tracks, looking at me to make sure he heard me correctly. "She's having your baby?" he verifies.

"Yeah, she's about sixteen weeks along," I tell him. "We'd only exchanged first names. She had no idea who I was, only found me because she recognized me when a game was on TV."

"And you trust her that this isn't some kind of trap or scam?" he asks. The questions sting, but I know he's coming from a good place. I've heard of countless guys getting scammed out of thousands because some chick claimed to be pregnant with their kid.

"I trust her one-hundred percent. Her dates line up

and, when it comes down to it, I just trust her. She's been through a lot already, her husband was killed in an accident, she was ready to hire a PI to find me because she felt it was that important that I knew about the baby and could decide for myself if I wanted to be in the child's life."

"And that's what you want, right?" he asks.

"One-hundred percent. Distance is going to be a pain in the ass, but I'll figure it out," I tell him as we push through the doors into the weight room.

"Well, if there's anything I can help with, just say the word. If you want my attorney's info, I can get that to you. He was really efficient with the custody and paternity stuff for Evie."

"I'm not sure it will come to that, but if it does, I'll hit you up, for sure," I tell him as I step onto a treadmill.

I put my earbuds in, cranking the speed up on the machine, and let my worries out on the belt of the treadmill as I pound out the miles.

Hannah

AFTER BREAKFAST, I GET BRAYDEN INTO THE BATH, then take a shower myself while he watches another show. Standing under the warm spray, my thoughts go to last night. How amazing Matt was when taking care of me. I was a little disappointed when he was dressed when I came out of the bathroom last night, but it was for the best. I don't need to jump back into his bed so quickly. I don't know what to expect or want to happen between the two of us, but I'm open to exploring things. If these hormones get their way, I'd jump into his bed all the time. Second-trimester hormones are no joke.

I get out of the shower and see that I've missed a text from Matt, so I quickly read it and reply.

Matt: I've talked to Carmen, she's the team's PR manager. I don't remember if I ever introduced you to her when we were on vacation, but she was one of the friends I was with. Anyway, she's going to be the one to get you two into the stadium. She just said to call or text her when you arrive, and she'll meet you at the doors.

He's attached her contact, as well, so I quickly save it to my contacts.

Hannah: Perfect, I'll get in touch with her when we arrive.

"All right, buddy, it's almost time to go. Let's get our shoes on," I call out to Brayden.

He quickly shuts off the TV and goes to find his

shoes. Once we're both ready, we head for the car. Since the parking at the stadium won't be an issue today, I just drive my own car over, unlike last night when we took an Uber.

"Matt is nice, I really like him, Mommy," Brayden says as I drive the few blocks.

I smile at his honesty. Kids tell it like it is, they don't hold back. It makes my mom heart happy that he likes Matt. It helps reassure me that having Matt in Brayden's life is a good thing. After Ryan died, I was worried about having a good male role model in his life to fill that dad-like figure. I'm not saying that Matt will do that, but it makes me comfortable with the idea that he could. Especially now that he's going to be Brayden's sibling's dad.

"I agree, buddy. He's a pretty nice guy. One that might be in our lives more. Would you be okay with that?" I ask him, starting to feel him out.

"Yeah," he easily agrees.

I pull into the parking lot, selecting a space close to the doors. I pull my cell out to send a text message to Carmen.

Hannah: Hi! This is Hannah, Matt gave me your contact to text when I arrived at the stadium. I just parked and am near what I believe is the main entrance.

The little dots pop up right away, so I wait for the reply to come through.

Carmen: Yes! I'll be right down.

"Okay, let's go!" I tell Brayden. "Don't forget your glove. Maybe you can throw a few balls with Matt."

He grabs his glove from the seat next to his booster before hopping out of the car. You'd think I was taking this kid to Disneyland with how excited he is to go and watch practice. His excitement level is even higher than it was last night before we went to the game.

"Hi, I'm Carmen," a woman greets as she pushes the doors open. "You must be Hannah, and this must be Brayden! It is so nice to meet the two of you."

"Hi, it's nice to meet you, as well. Thank you for getting us inside. Brayden has been looking forward to this all morning."

"I bet he has. Let me get you inside and down to the field," she says, holding the door open for us. We follow her inside the entry and through another door that I'm sure the general public never gets to go in. "This, here, is part of the team offices. It is kind of boring compared to downstairs." She chuckles as she leads us to an elevator.

A quick ride down and we're in another hallway. "This, here, is the clubhouse. Only accessible by the players, staff, sometimes the media, and invited guests," Carmen explains.

We stop at a little desk, and she picks up two lanyards. "These are for the two of you, they are your passes that allow you to move about. We don't have anywhere the amount of security here right now as we would have had during the game last night, but there are still a few that wander around or sit in specific places to make sure no one sneaks into the locker room to cause trouble for the players or coaches."

"Thank you," I state, sliding the lanyard over my head. Brayden does the same, checking out the badge that has his name printed right on it.

"I took the liberty to print you passes good for the rest of the season. I figured there might be a chance you'll be back," Carmen says, and I'm slightly embarrassed she knows why we're here. "Don't worry, your secret is safe with me," she says in a whisper so only I can hear.

"Thanks, I appreciate that," I tell her.

"I know how to spin a story. I've already talked to Matt briefly about how he wants to handle things with the press, but if you need anything at any time, you just call or text me and I'll be on it." The idea of my relationship with Matt or the news of our baby on the way being important enough that it needs a press release causes my anxiety to spike. I suck in a deep breath, willing my body to stay calm. It has been a long time since I've experienced a panic attack. I started getting them after Ryan died. It took many months with my therapist, working through the grief of losing my husband, for them to slow down and eventually stop.

"Thanks, the need for any and all of that has never crossed my mind, so I don't even know what to say."

"You don't need to say anything right now. Matt didn't want to do anything right away, or at least until he'd had the chance to talk to you. I just wanted to let you know that I'm here for you if you need anything or if the press finds you and starts bothering you."

"Thank you for that. I'm still a little overwhelmed that I actually found Matt. It has been a crazy couple of months."

"I can only imagine. Matt's a good guy, so you lucked out on that front," she says as we head out a door and into the seats. We're close to the field and make our way down to the front row. There are a few guys out throwing balls back and forth. Some others out running what looks like sprints, and some others by home plate setting up to hit balls.

"Look, Mom, there's Matt!" Brayden says, pointing out to the guys throwing the balls back and forth. He's bouncing up and down on the balls of his feet, the excitement pouring off of him.

"What a cutie," Carmen comments. "He seems like a great kid."

"Truly the best, and I'm not just saying that because he's mine."

"I'll be right back, I forgot I have something else to give him," she says, standing up and walking back through the door she led us out. I turn my attention back to the guys on the field. I've never been a huge sports fan, I'd watch a game here or there when Ryan was watching one, but I've never been obsessed myself. Now that I've got a front-row seat and can see all these guys this close, I can see why so many women love to watch baseball. The way these guys fill out the baseball pants should be illegal. It doesn't help my pregnancy hormones are running wild.

"Hey, you guys made it," Matt says as he jogs over to us.

"We did." My smile matches his.

"Do you want to come throw the ball with us?" Matt asks Brayden.

"Really? Can I, Mom, please?" Brayden turns his attention to me, practically begging to go.

"I suppose. You sure it will be okay? Your coaches won't mind?" I ask.

"They won't mind, I promise."

"Didn't your practice just start?" I question some more.

"It did, but we move around to stations, basically. Don't worry, I'm not going to get in trouble for bringing him out on the field. The guys with kids do it all the time."

"Okay, be safe, and listen to Mr. Matt," I instruct Brayden.

"Will do, Mommy!" he says, jumping around. Matt reaches over the railing and grabs Brayden under his armpits, helping to lift him up and over. I pull my phone out and open the camera up so I can capture this experience for Brayden. He's going to be talking about this for months to come.

"You must be Hannah." One of the other guys stops near the railing Matt came to a little bit ago.

"I am," I confirm. I have no clue who this guy is, other than someone else on the team. I'm sure if I was any other woman, I'd be falling all over this man. He's definitely a gorgeous specimen of a man.

"Sorry, I'm Justin, or JJ to most people," he introduces himself, holding a hand out for me to shake.

"Nice to meet you, Justin," I greet him, dropping my guard slightly. I couldn't tell right away how judgmental he was going to be. I have no idea if any of Matt's teammates know who I am or why I'm here. He hasn't had long to tell them, but that doesn't mean that he hasn't, seeing as how he already told the PR lady. I realize that she never returned with whatever it was that she was going to get, but that's perfectly fine as Brayden is more than enjoying himself.

"I admit, I'm not up on my baseball knowledge, so you'll have to forgive me that I have no idea who you are or what position you play."

JJ chuckles. "Matt wasn't lying, you are different. I'm one of the catchers on the team."

"Matt has talked about me?" I question.

"He told me about you this morning," JJ admits.

"Ah, and let me guess, you warned him I might be a gold digger that was trying to trap him?" I ask.

The tips of JJ's ears pinken ever-so-slightly, so I know I've pegged him. "It's okay, I expected that. To be honest, I somewhat thought that I would get that reaction from Matt himself. I'm glad I didn't, but I was prepared for it to happen," I tell him.

"I know all about surprise babies. My daughter's birth mom dropped her on my doorstep and walked out of her life. Unlike you've done, she never told me I was even going to be a dad, just showed up with a three-month-old and said, here, she's yours, I can't do this anymore, and that was it. I knew nothing – and I mean nothing about babies. They were never on my radar. I was the playboy of baseball, always getting in trouble with our coaches, and the press loved me, but that little girl changed my life and gave me my forever."

"Wow, that's quite the story," I say.

"It was. Not only did I get an amazing daughter out of the ordeal, but she led me to my wife, and now we have a son, as well. Life is crazy, but fate can do some amazing things. If fate is leading you to Matt, my advice is to go with it. He's an amazing guy and you'd both be lucky to have found one another."

Tears prick the back of my eyes at JJ's words.

"It was nice to meet you, but I've got to get back to work," he says as he looks over his shoulder and thumbs in the direction of some of the guys out on the mound.

"It was nice to meet you, as well," I call out to him.

I focus on Brayden and how the smile hasn't left his face as he moves around the baseball field with Matt. It amazes me how easily Matt shows him what they're doing at each of the stations as they move from one to another. He's soaking up every word these guys say to him. I don't know how I'm going to contain his excitement or knowledge that he's picked up today. How many other five-year-olds can say they got a private practice in with an MLB team?

The guys start dispersing from the field as they finish up. Matt and Brayden make their way back over to where I'm sitting, matching smiles on both of their faces.

"Did you have fun, buddy?" I ask Brayden.

"So much fun!" he exclaims, jumping up and down as he pumps his hand in the air.

"Thanks for letting him come out, we had a good time," Matt says, flashing those dimples that melt my panties right off.

"Of course, I don't think that I'd have been able to contain him in the seats, so it was probably in my best interest that I let him go."

"He definitely has a high level of energy," Matt states.

"You caught onto that, huh?"

"Yeah." He laughs with me.

"I need to go shower and change, then we can take that quick tour and get out of here for some lunch, sound good?"

"Sounds great. Should we just wait here?" I ask.

"Sure, unless you wanted to head inside?" he asks.

"What do you think, buddy? Wait here for Matt to come back or do you want to wait inside?"

"I don't care," he says, plopping down on one of the seats. I'm guessing he's exhausted after how much running around he's just done while Matt practiced.

"I'll be quick," Matt assures me before he takes off and heads for the locker room.

"I had fun watching you out there," I tell Brayden. "I got lots of pictures and videos. We can show Auntie Courtney when we get back home. She's going to love that you got to do that today."

"Can we FaceTime her?" he asks.

"Not right now, she's at work," I remind him.

"Oh, I forgot." He slouches down in a chair, sad that we can't call Courtney right this second.

"It's okay, buddy, no need to be sad, we can talk to her later when she isn't at work."

"Promise?" he asks, perking up a little bit.

"Pinky," I say, holding my pinky out to him to link and shake. "How about we send her a picture of the two of us right now, instead?"

"Okay," he says. He moves to standing next to me and I do my best to angle the camera so the field is behind us, getting some of it into the picture.

"Looks good," I tell him as I check over the image before sending it to Courtney.

Hannah: {picture of Brayden and mom} Just wanted to say hello! Brayden would like to FaceTime with you later today when you're free. He misses you.

Courtney: OMG the two of you are seriously the CUTEST EVER. And is that the stadium... on a weekday? Does that mean that you found him and are falling madly in love with him, running off to have some hot baseball player's babies and leaving me behind?

Hannah: Dramatic much? LOL {kissy emoji face}

Courtney: Way to avoid my questions.

Hannah: Yes, I've found him, yes, I've talked to him and told him about the baby. Yes, he's just as amazing and incredible as I remember him being. No, I haven't slept with him... but I have gotten some amazing kisses and the best massage ever. I'll dish more later, but he's coming back out from the locker room now, so I've got to go. Love you bye.

I put my phone in my pocket, standing as Matt approaches. "Are you guys ready?" he asks, rubbing his hand together? "I'm starving, so let's get this tour over so we can have some lunch."

"Sounds good."

"Come this way," Matt instructs, pointing down a little ways to another opening that allows field access.

Once we're all down on the field, he points out little things that the average person might not know. We head inside, and he shows us all over the clubhouse, the final stop being the locker room. Most of the guys have left, only a few still mill around. We walk over to the cubby marked with Matt O'Riley and he picks up a jersey laying across the bench. I realize right away that it's a kid's size, not adult. Once again, I feel tears prick the back of my eyes, these damn pregnancy hormones making me cry at the drop of a hat.

"I'VE GOT SOMETHING FOR YOU," I TELL BRAYDEN as we approach my locker. I had Carmen find me a kid's jersey and have it personalized while we were practicing. It's good to have connections sometimes.

"A jersey," Brayden gasps. "For me?" he asks, taking it from my hands and hugging it tightly.

"Yep, and it is signed by everyone on the team," I tell him, helping him turn it around so I could show him the back of it and all my teammates' signatures.

I wasn't expecting it, so I almost fall over when he crashes into my legs, hugging them tightly. I crouch down to his height, pulling him in for a real hug. "You're welcome, kiddo. I'm glad you like it," I tell him, and I can hear Hannah sniffling from beside us.

I turn my head to look at her, and sure enough, she's wiping some tears from her eyes. "Did you want a jersey? I wasn't sure if that was weird or something you'd like. If it is, just say the words and I'll have one down here in a few minutes, but I also didn't want you to feel obligated."

"I'm good; jerseys aren't usually my thing," she says, and I realize once she's declined the offer, how much I was hoping she'd take it, thus putting my name on her back. That feeling that she is my future is back in full force and I don't mind it one bit.

"What do you guys say we get out of here and head for Taco & Guac?" I ask. "A few of the guys and their families will also be there, so you'll get to meet a few more people," I say, more to Hannah than Brayden.

"Sounds good to me, I'm definitely ready to get some food in my belly," Hannah says, and now I'm worried I've kept her too long and am now starving her and my unborn baby.

"It hasn't been too long, has it?" I ask.

"No, but if you make me wait too much longer, I might turn into the Hulk with my hangry status," she says, and tries to hold in a laugh. She fails, and that sound is the sweetest I've heard in a long time.

"Then let's go!" I lead them out of the locker room and toward the parking lot. "Do you want to ride with me, or I can ride with you, and we can come back here later for my car."

"If it is more than a few blocks, I should take my car so Brayden can be in his booster," she says, and I don't know why I didn't think of that.

"Of course, let's just take your car and then come back later for me to pick up mine."

"Sounds good. I parked by the front office area," she says. "I have no clue how to get back to that parking lot, so hopefully you know." She laughs nervously.

"We're all good," I assure her, taking a left at the end of the hall so we can head back upstairs and out the front instead of into the staff lot.

Once in the car, I give her the directions to my favorite local place, Taco & Guac. I think it is a team staple to eat here. We often run into the guys from the Eagles here, as well. I'm sure the owners love that most of the professional sports teams in the city love their restaurant so much.

We park and head inside, finding JJ and Riley, Derek and Jillian, and Carmen and Lucas, all already seated around a big table. There are three seats left for us. Once we reach the table, I pull one of the chairs out, motioning for Hannah to take the seat before I help Brayden get settled. "Everyone, this is Hannah and Brayden."

My group of friends all gives them a warm welcome. I know some of the women are extremely curious about me showing up with a woman and a kid, and they'll learn more soon.

"Hannah, this is Justin, or JJ for short," I introduce him.

"We met at the stadium," she informs me.

"You did?" I ask, not aware that happened.

"Yep, I went over to where she was sitting and introduced myself. We had a nice little conversation."

"Alright, then, the woman next to him is his wife, Riley, who happens to be the next guy over's little sister – that's Derek and he's married to Jillian. Last but not least, this is Carmen, who you met earlier, and her boyfriend, Lucas."

"It is so nice to meet you all," she says to everyone, giving a little wave.

"How old is your son?" Jillian asks.

"He's five," she says as she reaches over and runs a hand over his head.

"Are you from around here?" Riley asks next.

"No, we live in Springfield," she answers.

"How'd the two of you meet?" Derek asks.

"In the Bahamas," I answer for her. "Back in December," I add. I can see the wheels turning in my friends' minds.

"Well, welcome. We're glad to have you here," Carmen says. "How long are you in town?" she asks.

"Thank you, I'm still a little overwhelmed by all of this. We're here just a couple of days," she says before glancing at me. I can see the questions in her eyes as she wonders how much she should say in front of my friends.

The question-and-answer session is thankfully interrupted when the server arrives at end of our table. Once we've gone around the table placing our order, another server shows up with baskets of chips and salsa to place around the table. The conversation flows smoothly the rest of our time. No one grills Hannah on what's going on, which I'm thankful for.

"Your friends are all so nice," Hannah says once we're back in her car and on our way back to the stadium so I can get my car.

"They're some of the best people I know. They've all been through their own unique situations. I can guarantee none of them will blink an eye at our situation."

"You know what I just realized?" she asks, looking at me quickly before turning her eyes back to the road.

"What's that?"

"I never once worried what they'd think. I don't know why, but I'm glad to know that they won't think I'm some random chick trying to trap you or just someone out looking to make a buck because of your job."

"That would be kind of hard when you didn't even know my last name or what my profession was."

"Exactly." She chuckles right along with me.

She pulls into the parking lot that I point her to; I hand her my badge to open the gate, giving us access to the secure players' lot where I park. "What are your plans for the rest of the day and tonight?" I ask. I'm not ready to not be around her and Brayden.

"I hadn't planned anything."

"Can you follow me home?" I ask. I have no clue

what we can do, but I just know I don't want today to end.

"Sure," she agrees, her eyes flicking to the rearview mirror to check on Brayden.

"I don't live super far," I tell her. "I'll put my address into your GPS just in case we get separated on the road." I tap at the screen on her dash, entering my address quickly.

"See you in a few minutes," I say before climbing out of her car and into my own.

I tap the screen on my own dash, the sound of a phone ringing immediately coming from the speaker.

"Yo, man, miss me already?" Derek asks, and I don't miss the laughter in his voice.

"Shut it. I need some help," I tell him quickly.

"Anything, what's up?"

"I'm on my way home, Hannah and Brayden are following me. I have no clue what to suggest we do for the rest of the day. Can you recommend something that a five-year-old would enjoy?"

"There's the children's museum or the zoo. My kids love both of those places. If you don't want someplace majorly public like that, there's always just hanging out at home, maybe heat up your pool for a few hours."

"Thanks, man, I'll see what Hannah thinks would be best."

"If you decided to head out somewhere and want some company, I'm sure I could talk Jillian and the kids into meeting up. We could probably wrangle JJ and crew to come, as well."

"I'll keep you posted," I tell him.

"I'm happy for you, man. She seems like a keeper."

"Yeah, things are complicated right now, but I hope it all works out for the best."

"We'll do whatever we can to help you. Just say the word," he says.

"Thanks, man. I really appreciate it. I'll let you know what we decide to do."

"Sounds good, talk to you later," he says before we disconnect the call.

I check my rearview mirror to make sure that Hannah is still behind me. A car has slid between us, but I can still see her so I'm not worried.

She follows me into my neighborhood. Instead of rolling through the resident lane since my car has a sensor that opens the lift gate for me, I roll through the visitor lane so I can tell the security guards that she's with me and to have them add her as an approved guest. It takes them a minute before they wave us both through. Some people complain about gated communities and all their rules, but I like having that extra layer of security.

"Wow," I hear Hannah say as she steps out of her car. "This is all yours?"

I look at my house, trying to take it in like she is. "Yeah, I bought it not long after being traded here. I hated living in apartments or condos. It was, hell, still is way more room than I need for just myself. But this is a really safe neighborhood and filled with some of my teammates, as well as members of the Indianapolis Eagles team. I don't have to worry about random fans just showing up on my doorstep or a random paparazzi."

"I don't know how you guys do it. To have everyone all up in your business like that. It was bad enough the few weeks I had to deal with the media frenzy when Ryan was killed. But like with most news-worthy things, it doesn't take long before the next big story hits and the previous one is pushed to the side and easily forgotten about."

"Some guys struggle with it more than others. I've always done my best to just ignore them. I realized that as long as I don't do stuff that spurs them on and makes me a target, they tend to leave me alone. I get a good laugh in when my mom calls me to tell me she's found my picture in the newest weekly magazine out shop-ping for something mundane like bananas or coffee."

"I can't even imagine." She giggles. "Matt O'Riley changes up coffee order, what that predicts...find out on page five." I can't help but get lost in her silliness and laughter.

"I'm pretty sure they've run that exact headline."

"You have got to be kidding me?" She laughs even harder.

"Nope," I pop the p. "Shall we head inside? I can

give you a quick tour and then we can make some plans for the rest of the day."

"Sounds good." She opens the back passenger door, then helps Brayden undo the seat belt.

He hops out of the car, his level of energy evident by the way he jumps around.

I lead them inside. We come in via the garage since I had the door open already from parking inside.

"Your house is gorgeous," Hannah compliments as we walk through the bottom floor.

"Thanks, I didn't pick out much of it, just the couch, TV, and my bed. Everything else my mom did with the help of an interior designer. I knew if it was left up to me, I'd only have those few items I'd picked out. I wanted this place to feel like home, so it was worth the money."

TWELVE
HANNAH

I KNOW PROFESSIONAL ATHLETES MAKE GOOD money, but damn, Matt's house is amazing. I think my entire house would fit inside his living room and kitchen. I can't believe he has all this house, and it is just him. I can understand wanting the security and exclusivity his neighborhood brings.

"Make yourself at home," he says. "Can I get either of you something to drink?" he offers.

"I'll take a glass of water if you don't mind. Brayden, are you thirsty?" I ask him.

"Yes, can I have some juice?"

"Let's go see what we can find," Matt says, holding his hand out to Brayden to take. I can't help but smile at how easily the two of them get along. I walk behind them as we enter the huge kitchen. It boasts stainless steel appliances that look like they've hardly been used.

A large island is in the center with six barstools tucked along one side. I pull one out and sit down.

"Would you like ice?" Matt asks, pulling down a glass from one of the cabinets.

"Yes, please."

He fills the glass with ice and water from the dispenser in the fridge door, then brings it to me, setting it down on the counter in front of me.

"Thanks," I say, flashing him a small smile.

"You're welcome."

He walks back to the fridge, pulling it open to see what he's got in there. "So, bad news, I don't have any juice, but I do have milk, Gatorade, or water," he tells Brayden.

"Can I have Gatorade, Mom?" he asks me. His puppy dog eyes out in full force.

"As long as it is okay with Matt, I suppose."

"Yes!" he cheers.

"I've got red, blue, orange, and yellow. Do you have a preference?" Matt asks him.

"Blue!" he says, and his excitement is contagious.

Matt pulls the beverage out and cracks the top open for him, handing over the bottle.

"Careful not to spill it," I remind Brayden as he brings the bottle to his little lips.

"So, on our way over here, I called Derek to get some ideas of kid-friendly things we could go do this afternoon. It's totally up to you, but I figured doing something would help the little man from going stir crazy."

"Oh, okay. What did he suggest?" I ask, a little shocked he's thinking so much of my son.

"He suggested either the children's museum or the zoo. If you don't want to go out in public, I can turn on the heater for the pool and we can go in that in a little while. Derek also said that if we wanted company, he could round up his family and meet us and probably rope in JJ and his family."

"I'm fine with whatever. Will you be bombarded with people if we go out in public?" I ask.

"That is hard to predict. I haven't been to either of those places, but it really comes down to if anyone recognizes me and how vocal they are about that on social media. I'd like to say that most people are respectful of our privacy—well, that is once they've gotten whatever items they have signed and a picture or two taken. But it also doesn't take long for someone to then post those pictures to social media and state where they were, and people will flood to that location to try and find us."

"It sounds exhausting. How do the guys with wives and kids keep them safe?"

"Most people are respectful of the kids. I can't recall a time that anyone was put in a dangerous situation. I'm sure it has happened, but none since I've been with the Lightning."

I worry my lip, not wanting to put us into any

sticky or potentially dangerous situations. On the other hand, this is something that I'll have to learn to live with if Matt does as he's said he liked to do and be in our lives once this baby is born.

"If it isn't too much trouble, I think going somewhere for a little while would be fun."

"Not a problem at all," he says, and places a hand on my shoulder, giving it a little squeeze to reassure me. "Hey, Brayden, can I take you somewhere fun today?" he asks him.

"Like where?" he asks from where he's perched next to me on one of the stools.

"Do you remember my friend, Derek?"

"The really tall guy that throws the ball a lot?" he asks.

"That's the one," Matt laughs at Brayden's description of Derek. "He has kids your age and said that the children's museum or the zoo are pretty cool places to go. Would you want to go to one?"

"Do they have monkeys?" he asks, perking up.

"I don't know, to be honest with you, I've never been. But I'm sure they've got some awesome animals we can check out."

"Okay," he says, and hops down from the stool. "Can we go now?"

"Give us a few minutes, okay, buddy?" I say.

"Okay." His little head turns down like asking him to wait just a couple of minutes is the worst thing in the world.

"I'm going to text Derek and JJ and see if they want to meet us there with their families," Matt tells him as he drops down to his haunches so he's down at Brayden's level. Little things like that make me believe he'd be the same way with our baby. I can already tell this man is going to be a damn good father. Our situation might not be a traditional one, but I can't think of anyone better that I'd want to be in this with.

⁓

"Mommy, look!" Brayden calls out as we stand at the Orangutans' exhibit.

"I see," I tell him as I take a short video of them playing around.

"They're just as crazy as my girls," Jillian says from next to me.

"I can only imagine. Brayden has always been so calm and laid back, but I'm sure having a built-in playmate changes that."

"It definitely does. My life is often chaotic, but I wouldn't change it for anything," she tells me.

"I'd always thought I'd have a houseful of kids. We were trying for another baby when my husband died. All my dreams went away when that happened," I find myself telling her, just as I realize I'm cradling my very tiny baby bump.

"Oh my, are you expecting now?" she whispers to me, obviously catching what I was doing.

"Yes," I answer her honestly. "It was a huge shock, one that I never dreamed of happening in a million years. Especially after a one-night stand." I can feel my cheeks burning with the embarrassment of our situation and sharing the details with Jillian.

"Everything happens for a reason. Derek and I divorced a couple of years ago. It was the wake-up call he needed to come back to me and our family. It was some of the hardest years of my life, but ones that I wouldn't necessarily give up because of what they did to bring us back together."

"Wow. I'd have never guessed with how he is with you and the kids. I know I haven't been around you much, but just know that what I have, you guys give off a very loving vibe."

"Thank you for that, but don't forget, what you see in public or on social media is only a fraction of our lives. His job might put him in the spotlight, but that doesn't mean that we're not still everyday normal human beings with normal problems. I still bicker at him to pick up his dirty socks, or to change the baby's diaper every once in a while."

As we make our way through the zoo, I'm amazed by how easily all of Matt's friends bring Brayden and me into their trusted circle. Not one of them raised a brow when they found out we were having a baby together.

"Drive safe and text or call me when you make it home," Matt says as he helps load our suitcase into my car. It's been two days since the day at the ballpark followed by the zoo. We've spent as much time together as we could with his schedule, and I've enjoyed getting to know him better.

"I will, I promise," I tell him, not sure what is an appropriate way to say goodbye to him.

"Come here," he says, reaching out and grabbing my arm. He pulls me into his arms, wrapping them tightly around my body. I slip my own arms around his torso, resting them on his back. He's all muscle, yet my cheek rests so easily against his chest, like it was made just to cradle me. We fit together like we were made for one another. "I'm going to miss having you guys here," he whispers, and I can hear the emotions in his voice.

"I'm going to miss you," I tell him honestly.

He tips my chin up and looks me in the eyes. I can see so many things when I look closely, so many unknowns. He lowers his lips to mine, giving me a chaste kiss. My hormones spring awake, but he doesn't push it.

"I'll be there in a few weeks, until then, we can call and text daily."

"Yeah, we've got some things to think about, don't we?"

"We do, but I have faith that we'll figure it all out in due time."

"I'm glad one of us is confident." I chuckle, trying to break the melancholy I'm feeling.

"Mommy, is it time to go now?" Brayden asks.

"Yep, say goodbye to Matt and then get in the car," I tell him.

Matt drops to Brayden's level like I've seen him do so many times these last few days. "Thanks for coming to see me, buddy. I had a great time. I'll see you soon, okay?"

"Okay," Brayden agrees as Matt pulls him into a hug. I have to wipe at the tears threatening to fall. Damn pregnancy hormones making me extra emotional.

"Can you make me a promise?" Matt asks him as they pull apart.

Brayden gives him a quizzical look, which causes both Matt and me to laugh at his expression. "Can you promise me that you'll be good for your mom and help her when she needs some extra help?"

He takes a moment to think things over, looking between the two of us before he finally agrees to Matt's request. "I'm always a helper, right, Mom?"

"The best," I agree with him.

"That's what I like to hear. Maybe when I come to see you, I can take you out for some ice cream or another special treat," Matt suggests.

"All right, we should get going," I say, to stop what I feel like is us just stalling the inevitable.

Matt and I stay back while Brayden climbs in and

buckles his seat belt. He's been learning how to do it all by himself. I have to remember he's not a little baby anymore. He's a big boy and can do so much on his own.

Matt pulls me in for one last quick hug, and I take the moment to just breathe him in. I still can't believe I found him and now have spent a few days together. "I'll miss all three of you," he says before letting me go.

I have no words, my throat feels like a bolder is in it, so I just nod in agreement. I didn't miss how he already included this little baby—our baby—in his sentiment.

I climb into my car, starting it before pulling my seat belt on. "I'll call or text you when we get home," I confirm before reaching for the door to close it. Matt steps up, grabbing the top of the door before leaning down so he can see inside.

"See you both soon," he says to both of us.

"Bye, Matt," Brayden says.

"Bye," I choke out, a few tears falling down my cheeks as the words leave my lips.

He lets go of the door, shutting it so we can get this over with.

THIRTEEN
MATT

The past few weeks have been strange. At moments, they felt like they'd never end, and others flew by in the blink of an eye.

I've been nervous but also excited that it is finally time for me to go to Springfield to see Hannah and Brayden, and of course, get to see my unborn child for the first time on an ultrasound machine.

Hannah and I have fallen into an easy rhythm. We talk daily. Sometimes that's by text, sometimes both text and FaceTime calls. But no matter what, we connect. She's told me about all the changes her body is going through, and I love seeing how much she's popped since she was in Indianapolis just a few short weeks ago. She's no longer able to hide the fact that she's pregnant. While I love what technology has given us, I hate not getting to see her in person. Getting those moments with her, feeling our baby grow, and helping her through all of this like a husband or boyfriend would.

Rather than waste time going home from our road trip, I booked a flight and flew straight to Springfield after our last road game. I didn't tell her, as I wanted it to be a surprise. As soon as I have my luggage, I order an Uber and head for the curb to be picked up.

"Holy shit, you're the real Matt O'Riley," my driver, Steve, according to the app, says once I slide into the back of his SUV.

"That I am," I confirm.

"I'm a big fan," he says before pulling away from the curb.

"Thanks, I appreciate it," I tell him. "I've got a marker if you'd like me to sign your hat," I offer, noticing that he's got a Lightning hat on.

"Yeah, man. That'd be great," he says, passing the hat back to me. I dig in my carry-on bag and pull out one of the many markers I've learned to carry so I can do just this.

"Anytime, and thanks for the support," I tell him as he makes it across town to Hannah's address.

"What are you doing in town? Don't you have a game later this week?" he asks.

"Just visiting a friend for a couple of days. Don't worry, I'll be back on the field before the next ball is thrown out," I assure him.

"That's good to hear," he says as he pulls into a neighborhood. It isn't anything fancy, but very middle class and appears to be a good part of town from what I can tell, seeing as how it's nighttime.

"Thanks for the ride," I tell Steve before sliding out of the SUV and grabbing my suitcase.

"Anytime, man, thanks again for signing my hat," he says, holding it up as he waves goodbye.

I walk up the walkway, stopping at the porch and knocking on the door. I don't want to ring the bell, knowing that Brayden is probably already in bed sleeping. I hope Hannah isn't also already in bed, seeing that it is almost ten.

Matt: Are you awake?
Hannah: Yes...why?
Matt: Open your door

I slide my phone back in my pocket and wait another moment until the front door cracks open.

"Matt!" she exclaims, opening the door all the way. "What are you doing here? When did you get in?" she asks.

I step inside her house, closing the door behind me. I can't help it; my hands go immediately to her round belly. I don't feel any movement, but I don't care. I move them, only to pull her entire body into mine and bury my nose into her neck. I take a moment to just breathe her in. I knew I missed her, but it really sinks in now just how much.

"I missed you," I tell her, pulling back to rest my

forehead on hers. It takes a whole hell of a lot of self-control not to pick her up and carry her to bed. What I wouldn't do to be inside her once again. It was the closest to feeling like I'd found my forever when we were together intimately all those months ago. "I caught a flight here instead of flying back with the team. Figured it would give me a little extra time with you."

"You should have told me; I would have picked you up."

"I didn't want to interrupt your evening or keep Brayden up late."

"Brayden isn't here tonight. He's with Courtney. They're having a sleepover at her house."

"So, it's just the two of us, alone?" I ask. I can hear the gruffness in my own voice as the question comes out.

"Yes," she says, her eyes dilating as she answers.

I suck in a deep breath, needing to rein in my hormones. "I need you to either tell me to leave and go find a hotel or show me to your room."

She pulls her bottom lip in, worrying her teeth on it for a moment. A moment that my cock throbs with the idea of those lips wrapping around it as she sucks me deep.

"I'm going to lay it all out on the line for you, Hannah. I want you. I want us. I hate this distance between us. I've never felt like I've belonged to someone until you. I also understand if you aren't on the same page as me. If you need me to step back, I will, but only where it pertains to pursuing you. I won't abandon you, or the baby. But my desire for you has only grown since that night in December. I thought I'd lost my chance when we went our own ways, but I believe fate had something to do with you finding me and bringing you back to me a few weeks ago."

"I-I feel it, too, Matt. I just need you to be careful with my heart. It's been shattered once; I don't think I'll survive if it shatters again."

"I can promise you; I'll never intentionally do anything to hurt you. I might mess up from time to time, I'm a man, it's what we do. But I'll also do everything I can to protect you and provide for you, Brayden, and this little nugget we created together."

"Okay," she agrees, and I pull her back into me. My lips find hers as my hands cup her cheeks.

"Please tell me it is safe for you to have sex while pregnant," I say against her lips.

"We're all good," she assures me. I don't need anything else. I slide my hands down her body, loving the way it feels, until I reach her ass. I cup the bottom of each cheek, lifting her up until she wraps her legs around me.

"Where's your room?" I ask, starting to head down the hall.

"Last door on the right," she tells me.

I make my way to the door, pushing it fully open and taking in the surroundings. I've seen it on Face-

Time, but this is my first time actually setting foot in this room. It reminds me so much of her. The way it is decorated. The way her scent fills the room floods my senses. I set her down on the edge of the bed and step back, pulling my polo shirt off over my head.

"It should be illegal how good you look shirtless," she muses, and I can't help but smile at her perusal and approval of my body. I've worked damn hard to keep in shape.

"What should be illegal is you not touching it."

"Cocky," she laughs. "I like it."

"I'll show you cocky." I unbuckle my belt, pushing my pants down, my boxer briefs along with them. My cock springs free, already hard, and ready for what's to come tonight. "Like what you see, sweetheart?" I ask, stepping closer to her as I palm my cock.

She bites her lip again and hums her agreement. "Yeah, I do."

"Then strip and join me."

She does just that, pulling the tank-top she had on off, followed by her shorts and panties. My mouth waters at the thought of getting to taste her again.

Once she's naked, I step up flush to the bed, between her legs. She's sitting up but is leaning back so she's resting on her elbows in a reclined position. I place a hand on either side of her body, boxing her in against the bed. I bring my lips to her ear, ready to tease the fuck out of her as I pleasure the fuck out of her.

"Ready to come for me, sweetheart?" I whisper as I drag my lips along the skin of her neck.

"Yes," she moans as I kiss my way down her body.

I take my time, exploring every curve, every inch of skin. "Are your breasts still tender?" I ask, looking up at her.

"Sometimes, it just depends on the day."

"Tell me if this isn't okay," I tell her before lowering my mouth to a nipple and lapping at it with my tongue.

"Ahh," she cries out, but when her fingers slide through my hair and hold my head to her breasts, I know that her cries are of pleasure and not pain.

I take my time, lavishing both breasts. They are much fuller than before, obviously changing with the rest of her body as she grows.

"Matt," she calls out my name and taps my shoulders. I release her breasts and glance up.

"What, sweetheart?"

"As much as I'm enjoying what you're doing, I need you inside me, now," she tells me. I had plans, but the woman gets what she wants.

"What's going to be most comfortable for you?" I ask, my hand cradling her belly.

"Umm, I hadn't really thought of that. I think the only positions that would work are spooning, me on top or you behind me."

"What sounds best to you?" I ask, wanting this to be good for her.

"All the above," she laughs.

"I'm good with giving all three a try," I say, dropping a kiss between her breasts before moving to lay down on the bed next to her. "Straddle me," I suggest, and help guide her as she does just that.

The moment her wet pussy slides along my length, coating it in her wetness, my body jerks to life. I've been hard since the moment I walked through the door, but I somehow harden even more. "Fuck," I groan as she slides up and down a few more times. I don't miss the way her breath catches each time my crown hits her clit.

Hannah lifts her hips up as she reaches down to grip my cock. I have to grit my jaw at the feeling of her fist wrapped around my shaft as she lines her opening up with my crown and sinks down inch by inch.

"Holy hell," she calls out. "So big, so tight," she moans.

"Fuck, you feel fantastic," I tell her, pulling her down so I can kiss her lips. She opens immediately for me, as we both deepen the kiss. My eyes about roll back in my head as she bottoms out, taking my cock as deep as she can. We still, our only movements happening from our deep kiss as she adjusts to my size.

I start to slowly roll my hips, matching the thrusts of my tongue with those of my cock.

Hannah pulls back from our kiss, sitting up and placing her hands against my chest for stability. I bring my hands to her hips and help her as she lifts her body up and down, bouncing on my cock.

"That's it, sweetheart," I encourage her. "Take what you need from me. Come on my cock."

"Yes," she cries out, and I can feel her body start to spasm.

Her movements slow, so I take over, pumping into her from below as I chase my own orgasm. It doesn't take long before I follow her over the cliff and empty everything I have into her.

Hannah falls forward, her belly pressed between the two of us as her head rests in the crook of my neck.

I run my hands up and down her back, enjoying the feeling of her in my arms.

She startles, sitting up, suddenly. "Did you feel that?" she asks, a huge smile on her face.

"I definitely felt you coming on my cock," I tell her.

"I know you felt that, but did you feel this?" she says, and grabs my hand, placing it against her belly.

I don't feel anything, at first, but a moment later, I feel pressure against the palm of my hand. "Holy shit," I whisper. "That's-" I find myself choking up with emotions. "That's our baby?" I finally get out.

"Yes," she confirms, smiling down at me as tears of her own fall down her cheeks. I wipe at them with my free hand, not wanting to move my other one from her belly anytime soon.

"We didn't hurt it, did we?" I ask, worried now that we've done something wrong.

"No, I'm sure the endorphins in my bloodstream have woken this little nugget up."

I can't help but laugh at her analogy. "I guess it's better than being walked in on by your kids."

"Right. At least this one we don't have to explain why Daddy has his private parts inside Mommy." She laughs, which causes the baby to move once again. I'm in complete awe of this moment and will remember this moment for the rest of my life.

"How long have you been able to feel the baby move?" I ask as she slides off of me, laying down next to me. We adjust our positions, my hand finding its way back to her belly where the baby was just a moment ago.

"I've felt butterfly-like movement, which is common to feel, at first. That is only on the inside. Yesterday, I thought I felt the first kick or punch from the outside, but it was so quick that I wasn't sure if I was imagining things. Then, today, the baby rolled and there was no missing it. I was waiting for you to call me tonight so I could tell you all about it."

"Even better, I got to feel it," I say before bringing her in for a tender kiss. "Thank you for this moment."

"I should be the one thanking you. I've had to rely on my battery-operated boyfriends a lot lately. This second-trimester hormones and sex drive are out of control."

"You definitely don't need to thank me for that. I'll gladly provide you with the cock to come on at any time."

"I'm sure you will." She smirks, kissing me again.

"How long do you need to rebound?" I ask as I slide a hand between her legs, finding her clit with my fingertips.

"Ah, I don't really know." She moans as I roll the bundle of nerves between my fingers.

"Think you can come just like this?" I dip two fingers inside her pussy, sliding them in and out at a lazy pace. I pull them fully out, circling the wetness around her clit before sliding them back inside as my thumb works her clit.

I love the way her body comes alive at my touch. The way she arches into me as her body seeks pleasure. "That's it, baby, find your cliff and fall. Let me catch you," I whisper between kisses to her neck.

"Matt," she cries out my name, her body convulsing as it squeezes my fingers tightly.

"You're so beautiful when you come," I tell her as she comes down from her second orgasm. "I could watch you all day."

"Sorry to burst your bubble, but I can't do that all day." She smiles as I kiss her lips.

"Smartass." I smirk, smacking her ass as she rolls into my side. The baby chooses that moment to start moving again and we lay there in wonder as we just feel all of it.

"Okay, I'm finally ready," Hannah says, coming down the hall. It's almost time to leave for her doctor's appointment.

"Let's go. Do you want me to drive?" I offer, even though I have no idea where we're going.

"I can, it's fine," she says.

I follow her out to the car. I love how much she has changed in the last few weeks, and getting to feel our baby move last night was an experience I can't even describe.

The drive isn't long, maybe ten minutes, at best. She parks and goes to open her door. I can't stop the nervous energy from coursing through my body, and I'm sure she can tell.

"Come on, now, let's go see our baby." She smiles over at me, and I want nothing more than to pull her into me and kiss her very kissable lips.

"You're sure last night didn't hurt the baby? Your doctor won't be able to tell what we did, will she?"

"No and I don't believe so, but even if they can, it is perfectly fine, Matt." She cracks a smile at me, obviously amused with my worry.

"I just don't want to be the reason either of you gets hurt."

"Stop worrying and let's go. I'm excited to see this baby and I need to pee but can't until after the ultrasound." Hannah grabs my hand and pulls me along with her.

After opening the door for her, I adjust my ball

cap, pulling it a little lower on my head to try and hide my face. I don't anticipate anyone recognizing me, but if they did and word got out that I was accompanying Hannah to an OB/GYN doctor's office, rumors would fly, and quickly.

We approach a receptionist's counter where Hannah fills out a slip of paper before handing it over.

"Good morning, Mrs. Knight," the receptionist greets Hannah. "Any changes with anything?"

"Nope, everything is still the same. However, I'd like to add someone to my account as an emergency contact and that can be given any information about my pregnancy or the baby."

"Of course, just fill out this form for me and we'll get your file updated."

"Thank you." She takes the form and clipboard from the receptionist.

"Go ahead and have a seat and they'll call you back in just a few minutes."

We do as instructed and take a seat in the waiting room. There are a few other women, most of them alone, but two have men with them. They are the most likely to recognize me, so I keep my head down and steer Hannah to a back corner, one where I might stay a little bit hidden.

"Can you fill in all your contact information for me, please?" she asks, handing me the clipboard. She's added my name, so I fill in all the pertinent information before handing it back so she can sign it. I watch as she takes it back up to the counter and hands it over. She says something to the lady and then returns to where I'm sitting.

"Everything okay?" I ask.

"Yes, I was just verifying they didn't need a copy of your ID or anything to go with the form," she tells me just as a nurse steps out of a door and calls her name.

We both stand, and I follow her to the nurse.

"Good morning, Hannah. Are you ready to see that baby this morning?" the bubbly nurse asks as she leads us down the hall.

"We are, and we'd like to find out the gender," she tells her, and then glances back at me with a look like she's verifying that I want to know that information. I give her a nod and a huge smile. I want to know any and all information I can about my unborn child.

"Right in here," the nurse says, pushing a door open and stepping in. "You can either change into this gown or just pull your shirt up and pull the band of your pants down to expose your belly, whatever you're more comfortable with."

"I can just move my clothes out of the way. I specifically picked this outfit as it's easy to move in."

"Perfect, just take a seat on the bed and the sonographer will be in shortly."

"Thank you," she says to the nurse.

I take a seat on one of the chairs next to the exam table, checking out everything that is in here. "What's the large TV for?" I ask.

"It is so we can see everything they're looking at."

"Oh, wow. I didn't think they'd be able to tell us much while we are in here. I figured we'd have to wait until we were in with the doctor."

"Nope. I think because the doctors here have such a great relationship with the sonographers, they trust them to tell the patient what they are looking at. It at least has been that way for any ultrasound I've needed since being a patient here."

"Good morning!" a cheery woman greets as she walks into the room. "How are we today?" she asks.

"We're great, just excited and maybe a little bit nervous to see our baby," Hannah tells her. I reach for her hand, linking our fingers together as the woman takes a seat.

"I'm Amy, and I'll be performing your ultrasound today. The nurse mentioned that we do want to find out the gender, is that correct? Do you want me to actually tell you or am I writing it down on a card so you can do a gender reveal at a later date?"

"We'd like to know today," I say, speaking up for the first time.

"Will do," Amy says. "I like to start with some of the standard measurements the doctors need, heart, kidneys, brain, etc. and then move to the lower body, unless the baby isn't cooperative and wants to show us its goods, first, which occasionally happens," she says, chuckling as she presses a few buttons on her machine.

Once she's ready, she squirts some gel on Hannah's

exposed belly and presses the ultrasound conductor to her skin.

"Baby looks great, so far, their head is measuring perfectly," she tells us as she takes some still images and marks down what I assume are the measurements she needs. "This, here, is the heart; it is also perfect and pumping blood just how we like to see."

"That's good to hear!" Hannah comments and my eyes flick to hers. She's got tears forming at the corner of her eyes, so I reach out with my free hand and wipe them away.

"You're doing great, Momma," I whisper in her ear before placing a kiss on her temple. I am in awe of this woman. Her strength is something even I can learn from.

"All right, guys, it's time," Amy says as she moves the ultrasound probe around Hannah's belly. "I just need the baby to roll slightly, and we can see what you're having. Can you roll onto your left hip, slightly?" Amy asks Hannah.

Hannah does as asked, and when Amy places the conductor back on Hannah's belly, her face lights up. "Perfect! All right, guys, this, here, is your baby's legs and that, there, is a vagina. Congratulations, it's a girl!" Amy says.

"A girl," Hannah gasps. "You're going to be a girl dad," she tells me, almost in awe and wonder.

"She's perfect," I tell her before I kiss her lips.

Seeing that we're in a doctor's office, I keep things PG and pull away after just a few seconds.

"I'll print out some pictures for you to keep, as well as a DVD that you can watch later, if you so desire."

"Thank you," Hannah tells her as she accepts the towel Amy offers and wipes at her belly, cleaning off the ultrasound gel.

"I'll get all these measurements to your doctor. You can head down the hall to exam room five. Go ahead and stop in the bathroom on your way and leave your sample, like normal," Amy instructs.

"Will do, and thank you," Hannah tells her.

I follow her down the hall. "Go ahead and wait for me in the room. I've got to pee in a cup for them and then I'll be in."

I do as instructed, and head into the room marked number five. I take a seat on one of the chairs and wait.

FOURTEEN
HANNAH

With my appointment over, we head out, huge smiles on both of our faces.

"I can't believe it's a girl," I tell Matt for probably the tenth time since finding out.

"Do you have any names picked out yet?" he asks once we're back in the car.

"Not really. My gut said that it was another boy, so I'd only been thinking of boy names the last week or so. Plus, I wanted your input."

"I'm just as clueless as you, but I'm sure we'll pick the perfect name for her."

"Are there any names that would have a tie to baseball that you'd want to consider?" I ask, knowing how important it is to him.

"Off the top of my head, no, but I can think on it."

"And I'll work on a list, and we can discuss."

"I did have something I wanted to ask you," Matt says as I pull back into my driveway.

"What's that?" I ask as I turn off the engine and turn my attention his way.

"Would you consider moving to Indy? Come live with me so we can see where this goes between us and allow me to be there to help you through the remainder of your pregnancy, as well as be around after she's born."

"I-I don't know what to say," I tell him honestly. "Can I think about it? As much as I want to say yes right away, I have so much to consider with that decision."

"I understand, and I'd expect nothing less. And if you decided that staying here is what's best for you and Brayden, I'll understand and we'll figure it out," he says, cupping my cheek.

My eyes start burning with that telltale sign that tears are forming. This man is so incredible, how caring he is. How he puts Brayden and my needs before his own. "Thank you," I tell him before leaning in for a kiss.

"Matt, stop." Brayden laughs as they wrestle on the living room floor. We've spent the afternoon and evening together, just the three of us, after Courtney brought Brayden back after we got home from my appointment. Having this time together today has been so nice, and makes me think of all the memories we could make together if I was to accept Matt's offer for us to move in with him.

"All right, buddy, how about we calm down for the evening. Maybe we can convince Mom to pop us some popcorn and curl up on the couch for a movie together, how does that sound?" I hear Matt say to Brayden.

"Popcorn," he says, popping straight up and running to secure his spot on the couch. I can't help but laugh at their antics, my heart full of so much love seeing my boy connecting so easily with Matt, and vice versa.

"What do you say, Momma, can we have some popcorn and a movie night?" Matt asks, turning his attention my way. I can't help but burst out laughing at his attempt at some puppy dog eyes.

"I suppose I can be talked into that," I tell him as I push off the couch.

He reaches his hand out, cupping my belly as I walk past where he's still sitting on the floor. "How are my girls doing?" he asks.

"We're good," I tell him. I can't help but smile even bigger at his sentiment. *His girls.* I could get used to that.

With a large bowl filled with popcorn, I grab a couple bottles of water and make my way back into the living room. I take a seat in the middle and place the bowl in my lap. "What are we watching tonight?" I ask.

"Brayden, have you ever seen the movie *Angels in the Outfield?*" Matt asks as he flips through Netflix.

"I don't believe he has. I haven't thought of that movie in years," I tell him honestly.

"As long as there's no objections, I think we've selected our movie to watch," Matt says, snagging a handful of popcorn from the bowl on my lap. He clicks around until he finds the movie available to stream and we settle in.

Once the popcorn is all gone, I find myself in a Matt-Brayden sandwich. I have two of my favorite guys on either side of me, both have moved closer the longer we sit here and watch the movie.

"Should I carry him to bed?" Matt asks once the movie ends. Brayden has fallen asleep and is passed out cold.

"If you don't mind, I can't pick him up with this belly in the way anymore."

He easily scoops him up in his arms, the ease at which he does that makes him a natural. I follow him down the hall and into Brayden's room. I click on a night light, basking the room in a low glow of light. I grab a pair of PJs from the dresser, then sit on the edge of the bed and get to work on changing him.

"Love you, Mommy," Brayden sleepily tells me, and my heart squeezes tight.

"Love you, too, buddy. I need you to go potty before I tuck you into bed," I tell him as I help him stand. Slowly and sleepily, he makes his way to the bathroom and quickly does, then brushes his teeth. Once he's done, he comes back to his room and climbs up into the bed. I pull the covers up and tuck them in around him. "Night, sweet dreams," I say as I kiss his forehead.

I click the light off before heading to the door. I glance back at him, taking in his sweet slumber. My baby boy is growing up so fast. The knowledge that he's going to be a big brother in just a few short months hits me, and I find myself crying as I watch him sleep. I finally had to break down and tell him about the baby a few weeks ago when I could no longer hide my growing belly. He was over the moon when I told him. He asked a few questions but was mostly just excited. When he got home earlier, I got to tell him that he'd be getting a sister. I thought he might be sad, wanting a brother more than a sister, but he blew me away with how excited he was about a sister being on her way.

"Come here, sweetheart. Why are you crying?" Matt asks as he slides up behind me. His arms go around my body, landing on my belly. I've noticed today that he gravitates to me. If he's within reaching distance, I think he's had his hand plastered to my belly, just hoping to feel her move again.

"Damn pregnancy hormones again. I was just thinking about Brayden no longer being my baby, no longer being an only child. The tears just hit me like they so often do lately."

"He'll always be your baby, no matter how many

more kids you are blessed with," Matt tells me, which does not help. I turn in his arms and bury my face in his chest, my tears falling even faster now.

"Shhh, shhh, everything's going to be okay, sweetheart." He consoles me, rubbing his hands up and down my back. "Let's go lay down, it's been a long day and you could use some sleep."

Matt leads me to my bedroom, and after he closes the door, I let him help me strip my clothes off and slip into some PJs. I excuse myself to the bathroom, once again needing to pee. This baby girl has definitely found her home directly on my bladder. I finish up with my nightly routine, brushing my teeth and applying some moisturizer.

When I exit the bathroom, Matt is already in bed, propped up against the headboard. I take a second to take him in. He's so easily slid into my life, establishing his importance.

I sit on the edge of the bed so I can take my watch off and place it on the charger on my nightstand. I verify my cell is plugged in and charging, as well, before I roll over and snuggle up to Matt. I've only slept next to him a couple of times, but I could sure get used to it. His question from earlier comes to the forefront of my mind. It would be a huge change for us; how I'd ever deal with moving from the home I created with Ryan, moving away from Courtney, my best friend and Brayden's aunt. It would be a huge change, but I also wonder what I'd be missing if I didn't take that leap of faith and at least see what happens.

"A penny for your thoughts," Matt says, pulling me from my racing mind. I slide a hand across his bare chest, still learning the feel of his body under my touch. "I can practically hear your mind racing tonight," he says, filling the silence.

"I have so much on my mind, but I'm mostly thinking about what you asked earlier today. Going over all the pros and cons of moving versus staying here," I tell him honestly. If we're going to pursue a relationship, we have to be honest and communicate. It is key in any relationship.

"I had an idea, it might be crazy, but might help make things easier," he says, and I'm all ears.

"What's that?" I ask, and shift so I can look up at him and see his eyes.

"What if we asked Courtney to move with you. My house is big enough for all of you to move in. She can have the guest master, which is on its own hallway. She'd have space to get away from everyone else, or if she didn't want to move into my house, I could find her an apartment or condo close by."

"You'd be okay with that?" I ask, shocked just a little bit.

"I wouldn't offer if I wasn't, plus, I know how much she means to the two of you. I hesitated to even ask you to move because I know how hard it would be for you to move away from your home, and everything this place represents, but also because your family is here. But if she could come and was willing to come, then I thought it might help you decide to do it."

"I'll definitely keep the offer in mind and ask her," I tell him.

"That's all I ask," he says before cupping my cheek and pulling me in for a kiss. It starts chaste but doesn't stay that way long.

FIFTEEN
MATT

I walk out onto the field, turning my head side to side as I stretch the muscles out. I caught an early flight today to get back for practice. It beat having to come back late last night, plus, gave me a few extra hours with Hannah and Brayden.

"You made it," JJ says as he tosses a ball in the air.

"Did you think I wouldn't?" I ask, and grab a ball of my own from a bucket.

"No, just wasn't sure how early you'd be here. How'd things go?"

I can't hide my smile, the last thirty-six or so hours I got to spend in Springfield were just what I needed. "It was good, really good," I tell him honestly. "Surprised Hannah when I arrived a night early. She surprised me with the fact that Brayden was spending the night with his aunt, so we had the night and morning alone," I tell him, my smile getting bigger as my mind replays our night together.

"That's my boy." He smirks, smacking me on the shoulder.

"Yeah, it was a good night," I confirm without spilling any of the details. "Then, we had her appointment. That shit was wild. Did you go to any of Riley's appointments or ultrasounds?" I ask.

"I didn't miss any of them. After missing all of that with Evie, I made sure I didn't miss anything this time around."

"When they turned on the sound for her heartbeat, damn that was something else. I recorded it on my phone so I can listen to it whenever I want."

"I did the same thing," he admits.

"So, a girl? Congrats, man."

I feel my cheeks heat, kind of a weird time to blush, but whatever. "Yeah, I'm joining the girl dad gang."

"We sure make a lot of them around here, must be something in the water." He laughs.

"Maybe," I murmur.

"When do you get to see them again?"

"A few weeks, I think. I actually asked Hannah to move here. Asked her to move in with me."

"Damn, and what did she say?" he asks.

"She's considering it. I know it was a lot to ask of her, but fuck, I just want her with me. Having two nights to hold her in my arms, playing with Brayden yesterday afternoon and evening." I pause, thinking back over my day with them. "It just felt natural and like I was finally settled."

"Hey, man, I'll be the first to admit that when it's meant to be, it will be. You know how I was, and look at me now. I never dreamed of being a dad and husband, and now I wear both of those titles with pride."

"I got to feel her move. It was the most surreal thing I've ever experienced," I tell him, but leave out the details surrounding that first movement.

"It's pretty cool, isn't it?" he asks, his own face lighting up.

"Yeah, it wasn't super strong, but Hannah had only just started to feel movement, as well."

"Just wait a few more weeks when the baby starts to run out of room. Her entire belly will shake when the baby moves. I'd sometimes put the remote on top of Riley's stomach, only to watch it be kicked off. It was pretty funny shit," he tells me.

"I'll have to try that next time," I tell him, liking the idea already.

"So, is she moving here?"

"I'm not sure yet. When I left this morning, she was still processing my question. Late last night, I even offered to have her best friend and sister-in-law move in with her. She really liked that idea, so we'll see what she decides here, soon."

"You must really like this chick if you're willing to have her friend come along, as well."

"She's been through a lot in her life. If having her

best friend close by helps, then I'm all for it. When her husband was killed, it was Courtney who stepped up and helped her with everything. I can understand not wanting to leave that kind of support system."

"I'm happy for you, man. Hopefully, she comes through with the move."

"I can only hope," I tell him before Coach comes out to tell us a few things before practice officially starts.

I fall into bed, dead-ass tired after my whirlwind trip to Hannah's, followed by a morning practice and an evening game. My body is beat and ready for a good night's sleep in my own bed.

After the game ended -- another win for us, I hit the showers and then spent some time in with the trainers, getting stretched out and some tight muscles worked on. Because my mind was focused on after-game shit, I never checked my phone. I finally take a moment to check it now and see that I've got a few texts and a missed call from Hannah.

My mind immediately jumps to something being wrong. My heart rate picks up, practically beating out of my chest while I listen to the phone ring.

"Hello," a sleep-filled voice answers the phone. "Matt?"

"Hey, sweetheart. I'm sorry I woke you. I just now checked my phone and panicked when I saw missed calls and texts from you."

"That's okay. I fell asleep on the couch, apparently," she says as I hear her yawn. "You had a good game."

"I did. Did you watch all of it?" I ask, a little excited at the idea that she's purposely watching my games.

"Of course, I did. Brayden, too."

"You must have been my good luck charm."

"I don't know about that..." She trails off, but I cut her off.

"I haven't played like that in years, and the only thing different between the last game and tonight was seeing you," I tell her.

"If you say so. Aren't baseball players superstitious?" she asks.

"They can be, why?" I ask.

"Just checking if this means you're going to be starting some new ritual before all of your games."

"I could definitely start a ritual of seeing you before my games. I like that idea a whole lot."

"I walked right into that one," she smarts.

"Did you talk to Courtney today, or think any more about my offer?" I ask, hopeful that she's ready to say yes to moving here.

"I did start discussing it with Courtney. She was intrigued by the idea and offer."

"That's better than a flat-out no."

"Yeah, I really do like the idea of her coming with. I just don't know how I'd survive with her a few hours away. Especially without knowing anyone but you there, no offense to you," she quickly adds.

"None taken," I assure her. "But you won't be alone here. My friends and their wives and girlfriends are more than ready to welcome you into their circle. Riley, Jillian, and Carmen are some of the best women I know. Add in a few of my buddies that play for the Eagles and their wives, and we've got quite the group here. The bonus is, all these women will know what it's like to be with a professional athlete and can help you deal with anything that arises because of that added spotlight."

"About that spotlight, are you wanting to make some kind of announcement about the baby?" she asks.

"I say we keep it to ourselves for as long as we can. I don't want to put any additional stress on you by announcing it. Since we haven't been linked in the media, I don't think that will happen."

"Thank you, I was nervous about that."

"Hannah, we don't ever have to do anything you're not comfortable with. I just need you to be open with me about what and where your comfort level is at. Can you promise me that?" I ask.

"Yeah, I'm just still a little overwhelmed, but I promise I'll talk to you. But the same goes for you, I need to know what you're thinking and feeling about things."

"I'll always be open and honest with you. One of my biggest pet peeves is dishonesty or when people hold back information because they're scared about something. Just get it all out there and we can work through whatever it is."

"It sounds like we're on the same page, then," she says, and I can hear her moving around.

"How are my girls tonight? Did you have a good day?" I ask, changing the subject.

"It was a good day. I started flipping through a baby name book."

"Did you find anything you liked?" I ask.

"I wrote down two names, but I'm still on the fence about them."

"Well, don't keep me hanging, what did you write down?"

"Brooklyn and Beatrice. I know Beatrice is kinda old school, but I love the idea of calling her Bea, for short. I also really liked it because it means bringer of joy. If she's done anything, it is to bring so much joy to my life and she isn't even born yet."

"I really like that," I tell her. "I haven't thought of any names yet, but I'll try and get a list going."

"We've got plenty of time," Hannah chuckles. "Well, hopefully about twenty more weeks, that is."

"Keep that baby in there growing, please."

"I'll do my best."

"That's all I can ask. Is there anything I can do from here?"

"Not really, but if I think of anything, I'll let you know."

"I really hate being so far away from you," I tell her honestly. "When can you and Brayden come out here again?"

"I guess we could come out later this week. I plan to let my boss know tomorrow that I'm quitting. I don't need the money to survive and the hours on my feet just aren't worth it."

"I agree. Besides your next doctor's appointment and your next few shifts, are they the only things holding you there?"

"Well, besides the rest of our lives, yes."

"I have an idea," I say, pausing to think it through before speaking it into the universe.

"And that is?" she asks, and I can just picture her using her hands and rolling them like she's motioning for me to get it all out.

"What if you came out next week and stayed until your next doctor's appointment. That will give you a few weeks to see if you like it here and could see yourself living here without the full commitment of a move. I'm sure Jillian or Riley could get you in contact with their doctor, so you can see if they'd be a good fit for you if you decided to move here permanently."

"I do like that idea. Let me think on it tonight and I'll get back to you tomorrow."

"I can live with that." A yawn slips out as my exhaustion level goes up.

"It sounds like you need to get to sleep, as do I, so

how about we call it a night and talk tomorrow?" Hannah suggests.

"Sounds good, sweetheart. Sweet dreams and call me in the morning. I won't be heading into the stadium until around ten or so."

"Okay, sleep well."

"Only thing better would be to have you in bed with me," I say.

"Charmer." She giggles. "Good night, Matt." Her sweet voice fills my ear before the line disconnects.

I roll over and plug my phone in before setting it on the nightstand. With it settled, I pull the sheet and blanket up and quickly fall asleep.

SIXTEEN
HANNAH

"Don't you worry one bit about me or anything here, I've got it all under control," Courtney assures me as we sit on my couch. She's going to house sit for me while Brayden and I go to Matt's for the next few weeks. His idea was actually a really good one. It will give all of us a trial run of what it would be like if we moved there permanently.

"I'm going to miss you so much." I pull Courtney into a hug, tears already streaming down my cheeks.

"That's what FaceTime is for. Plus, I have a feeling that man of yours is going to keep you nice and busy." She smirks. "Or maybe naked and well taken care of." She bounces her eyebrows at me.

"Stop." I cry-laugh, wiping at my tears. "I still have to be a mom, and he still has a job."

"Semantics." She shrugs. "And I'll be there before you know it," Courtney reminds me.

She's coming out for a long weekend in three weeks, to check things out and see if she'd be interested in moving if Brayden and I decided to make it a permanent move.

"I know, I've just never been away from you for so long," I remind her, new tears falling from my eyes. *Damn pregnancy hormones.*

"A few nights' worth of orgasms and you'll forget all about missing me."

"I could never forget you," I state, and that is the ultimate truth.

"All right, let's get you on the road," Courtney calls out a little while later. I've dried up my tears -- for now, at least.

"Bye, Auntie Court," Brayden says, running into Courtney's open arms. "I'm going to miss you," I hear him tell her. So much for my dried-up tears.

"I'm going to miss you so much," she tells him.

"How much?" he asks.

"To the moon and back."

"Wow, that's a lot," he says.

"It sure is, but that's how much I love you. But I need you to do me a favor, can you do that?"

"What?" he asks.

"I need you to be the best boy for your mom. She's a little bit sad about leaving, but I know that you'll both have the best time, and Auntie Court will be there in just a few weeks, so I expect you to be able to show me all the cool stuff there."

"Okay, can I FaceTime you?" he asks.

"Of course!" she says. "How about you plan to FaceTime me tonight. You can show me your bedroom and all your cool stuff, how's that sound?"

"Great!" he exclaims.

"Perfect. I'll expect a call before bedtime." She winks at him. "Why don't you go in and go potty and then go get in the car," she instructs him.

"Okay," he agrees.

"So going to miss you," I say again.

"Only a few weeks, you've got this. You're a great mom and just think of all the help Matt will be."

"I know, it is just weird. Don't get me wrong, I've learned so much about him these last few weeks, but it also feels like we've known each other forever."

"Sometimes fate has a funny way of working things out. Just go with it. See where this goes. This just might be your second chance at forever and I'm so happy for you that it is."

"I sometimes feel guilty that I'm moving on from Ryan," I tell her honestly, and it guts me to do so.

"Honey, if I know anything about my brother, it is that he loved you to the bottom of his soul. He'd want you to be happy and find love again. He might have been a big brute who was possessive, but I also know he'd step back if he knew that it would make you happy. You met Matt on one of your memorial trips, maybe Ryan sent him to you knowing that you needed that little push to move on."

"I sure hope you're right," I tell her, and blow out a big breath. The emotions from the last few days are catching up to me and the last thing I need is to be tired when it's time to get on the road and drive for the day.

"Enough sappiness, you need to dry those tears and get your ass on the road. Do I need to send you in for a potty break like I did your son?" Courtney asks with a smirk on her lips.

"Yes, Mommy," I smart at her.

I head for the bathroom because, hello – I've got a baby sitting directly on my bladder and I have to pee every hour it seems like some days.

"All right, we're ready!" I call out and head for my car. Brayden is already in the back seat, buckled into his booster seat. He's got his iPad in his lap and already playing a movie we downloaded. "You ready, buddy?" I ask.

"Ready!" he calls out and gives me a thumbs up.

"I'll keep you updated on our progress. Hopefully, we only have to stop once since it's only a little over three hours to get there."

"You better keep me posted, or at least let me know you made it there."

"I think we're having lunch as soon as we arrive, but I'll at least shoot you a text," I tell her as I pull my phone out and shoot Matt one.

Hannah: About to get on the road. Hoping

for only one stop, if possible, for a bathroom break.

Matt: Drive safe, sweetheart. I've added your vehicle info to my approved list, so you can go through the residence line when you arrive. If I'm not home, you can go on in and make yourself comfortable. I'll get your bags inside once I make it home.

Hannah: Okay, see you in a few hours.

I put my phone in the holder on my dash and turn to give Courtney one last hug. "I'll talk to you later. Thank you for everything."

"Drive safe, I love you," she says and hugs me tighter for one last second.

"Love you, too," I tell her as I slide behind the wheel and get myself buckled.

With Brayden engrossed in his movie, I crank up the tunes and drive to our new future.

SEVENTEEN
MATT

THE PAST COUPLE OF MONTHS HAVE FLOWN BY, we're already in the playoffs and hoping to make it all the way. Hannah and Brayden's three-week trip never ended. By the time Courtney came to check things out, we had settled into a nice little routine and none of us were willing to give it up. Hannah was able to transfer her maternity care here, getting in with the OB/GYN that both Riley and Jillian have used for their pregnancies.

"Hey, Momma, how are you feeling?" I ask Hannah, handing her a cup of crushed ice from the machine down the hall. We've been at the hospital now for five hours and she's progressing slowly but surely.

"Tired," she says and scoops a spoonful of the ice chips into her mouth.

"Do you want to take a nap?" I ask, feeling a bit helpless right now.

"Maybe," she admits.

I move a few of the pillows on her bed and help her roll onto her side. It seems like she's been the most comfortable when laying like that, so hopefully, that helps her get a little nap in before our daughter arrives.

"Matt!" Hannah screams out, waking me from a dead sleep. I, apparently, nodded off after she did, but that blood-curdling scream has me on my feet and by her side.

"I'm right here, sweetheart," I assure her, wiping her forehead off with a wet washcloth.

"I have to push," she cries as the monitor starts going off. I look up and see she's got a big contraction happening and it appears the baby's stats are falling the longer the contraction goes on.

Before I can find the call button to get someone in here, her door flies open and in comes two nurses.

"I was just fixing to call you. She just woke up and is in a lot of pain, says she's got to push."

"Can you roll on your back, sweetie, I need to check you quick," one of the nurses says. Once the contraction ends, I help get Hannah on her back and into place so the nurse can check.

"You are definitely ready; I can already see the top of her head," the nurse tells us before turning to her co-worker. "Can you get the doctor in here now; we don't have much time before this baby is going to be out."

The second nurse goes running out of the room, hopefully in search of the doctor. "I need you to breathe through your next couple of contractions, but don't push. If you push before the doctor gets here, you might deliver without her."

"I don't know if I can stop that from happening," Hannah cries out as another contraction hits.

Between the pained look on her face and the death grip on my hand, I know she's in pain and there isn't a damn thing I can do about it.

"You're doing so good, baby. You're a badass and the strongest woman I know. Our daughter is going to be so lucky to have you as her mom and a role model," I whisper as I run a hand through her hair and do my best to try and relax her.

"I don't know if I can do this," she tells me, and the fear on her face breaks my heart into a million pieces.

"You've got this, babe. You can and you will do this," I assure her. "Just think of the reward. We will finally get to meet our daughter. Get to finally pick what her name is going to be." Hannah could never narrow any of our lists down to one. She said she wanted to meet our little bundle of joy before picking one.

"Let's get this baby out!" Hannah's doctor says as she waltzes into the room.

I watch as she puts on a gown, gloves, and a face shield before sitting on the stool at the end of the bed transforming it into a delivery bed with little foot gadgets and other things I've never experienced before in my life.

"When I count to three, I want you to take in a huge breath and push as you blow out. We're going to do that a few times and, by then, we should have a baby, sound good?" the doctor asks.

"Okay," Hannah warily answers.

"You're doing great, Hannah," one of the nurses tells her. "Can you hold up this leg for her?" the other nurse asks me. I do as I'm asked and hold up one of her legs, just like the nurse on her other side is doing.

"Here comes a big one, deep breath in and ten—nine—eight—" The doctor counts her down, all the way to zero. "Good job, now relax," she instructs.

Hannah sags into the bed, I can see how exhausted she is getting.

"You're doing great," I assure her, wishing I could trade places with her and take all the pain away.

"Here's another one, get ready," the doctor calls out. Hannah opens her eyes as the nurse and I lift her legs back into position. She pushes with all her might and the most beautiful sound I've ever heard fills the room—the first cry from my daughter. *I'm a dad.*

"Congratulations, it's a girl!" the doctor calls out as she sets the baby down on Hannah's chest. She's covered in white stuff and crying like she's just been through something traumatic. "Would you like to cut the cord, dad?" the doctor asks me.

"Yes," I tell her, accepting the special scissors and doing just that.

Once the cord is cut, I turn my attention back to

my girls. Hannah is staring lovingly at our daughter, an expression of complete love on her tired face.

"You're a rock star." I interrupt the moment and kiss Hannah. "I love you," I tell her for the first time ever. She's given me the best gift I could have ever asked for. It isn't that I've not thought those exact three words for months -- because I have. I didn't want to scare her off by saying them too early.

"She's perfect," Hannah agrees with me, turning her attention back to the baby on her chest. She runs a hand over her head. It's covered with a small amount of peach fuzz-like hair. I've read about it in the baby books I've spent the last few months reading during my downtime.

⁘

"Brayden, can you grab your sister's binky and come with me?" I ask him quietly.

We've been home from the hospital for a couple of days already and I can tell Hannah is exhausted. She didn't get much sleep when in the hospital, and little Beatrice – or Bea, as we've all taken to calling her these last few days -- has been cluster feeding.

Hannah is finally sleeping, so I'm taking the baby and going into full dad mode.

"Can I hold her?" Brayden asks once we're out in the living room.

"Yep, just sit back and grab the pillow," I instruct.

He does as told, and I place Bea in his lap. He's really taken to his big brother role, and I love knowing that my daughter has such a great big brother in her life.

Brayden holds her until she starts to squirm a bit. "Matt, you can take her now," he says. I quickly scoop her up, bringing her to my chest and holding the binky in her mouth to see if that will satisfy her, for now.

"Hey, beautiful girl," I coo at her. "How's Daddy's baby? You sure have been keeping Mommy awake at all hours of the day and night. What do you think about letting her get some sleep, huh," I find myself babbling to Bea.

"Can I watch a movie?" Brayden asks. I check my watch, it's only three in the afternoon, and it isn't like we have anywhere to be tomorrow.

"Sure, did you have something in mind?" I ask him. He grabs the remote and turns the TV on, settling on one of the *Cars* movies.

Bea is content with the pacifier and quickly falls back to sleep on my chest. It is that exact position that Hannah finds us in an hour and a half later. Brayden curled up next to me on the couch, watching the end of his movie, and me enamored over our sleeping daughter on my chest. Life couldn't get much better than this.

"What's going on here?" she asks. I hold out my free hand for her to take, then tug her to sit down on my free side. She does so, and places a hand on Bea's back, not able to resist touching her when this close.

"Just relaxing. How was your nap?" I ask.

"Incredible. I almost feel human again."

"Why don't you go take a shower, it will make you feel even better," I suggest.

"That's the best idea ever." She leans in and gives me a quick chaste kiss.

"I know, that's why I suggested it." I smirk. "Love you," I tell her, as I've been doing since that moment just after Bea was born. She hasn't said it back, but I know she does. She's just struggling with it, and I get it, I really do. I don't need those three little words to know that she, in fact, loves me. I can see it in the way she looks at me or the baby. I can see it in the way that she trusts me with her son, and in the way she picked up her entire life and moved a few hours away to be with me since I couldn't really do the same.

EIGHTEEN
HANNAH

I sit in the living room, Bea in her swing after she nursed for the last half hour, filling her little belly all the way up. Matt and Brayden—my guys, as I like to call them—play a game together.

Bea is two months old already; time really needs to slow down. I still can't believe this is my life. How far I've come in the last few years. Going from feeling like I had it all, to rock bottom when Ryan died, back to the top when I met Matt, and then found him again.

Bea is truly our gift, she is the reason we found one another again, and for that, I will forever be grateful.

"Hey, beautiful." Matt pulls my attention from where my mind had wandered off to. "How's Momma holding up today?" he asks. He's been super attentive and helpful since she was born. Hell, before she was born, he was just as attentive, making sure I had everything I needed and then some.

"I'm perfect, how are you?"

"Never been better," he says before dropping a chaste kiss to my lips. He likes to do that whenever he gets the chance. I can't say I don't like it, because I absolutely do. "I was thinking, maybe we could ask Courtney to watch the kids tonight so I can take you out, what do you think of that?" The look of hope on his face has me caving in very quickly.

"I'm sure that could be arranged, what did you have in mind?"

"Some dinner and then whatever the night brings us after that." He winks at me. I know exactly what that wink indicates. This poor man has been so patient with me as I heal up after giving birth. I was given the all-clear for sex again at my appointment a little more than a week ago, but it just hasn't been the right time.

"I guess some celebrating is in order. We haven't properly celebrated your big win from earlier this month." The Lightning won the World freaking Series. That was surreal to watch. I loved every minute of cheering the guys on and being part of Matt's cheering section.

We were successful with keeping our relationship on the down-low until shortly before Bea was born. Once news broke, it was a crazy few weeks, but, thankfully, things have gone back to normal. I think it helps that we're not flashy people and out and about all the time. Having a newborn is a good excuse to stay pretty close to home most days. A cluster feeding baby makes it hard to get out much, so, thankfully, our friends have been more than willing to come to us.

"Whenever you're ready, sweetheart, no need to rush things if the timing isn't right," he assures me, and my heart melts all over again at how amazing this man is to me.

"I think tonight is perfect," I tell him. The way his eyes turn molten has my panties melting right here on the couch. How I'm going to make it until after dinnertime, I have no clue.

"You ready for that dinner, now?" he asks, pretending to check his watch that isn't on his wrist.

"What are we, eighty and hitting up the afternoon dinner rush?" I tease him. "It's only three thirty. You feed me now and you'll have to just do it again later."

"I'll feed you, don't you worry one bit." He smirks and I walked myself right into that comeback.

"You're so bad." I can't help but laugh at his comeback. "But I will take the D," I smart back at him.

"Woman, there are impressionable kids in this room," he says, like I'm not aware of them.

"The only one that even has the slightest idea we're even over here talking isn't paying one ounce of attention to us, and the other one is passed out in a milk coma. I think we're fine and haven't corrupted the kids yet."

"Can I corrupt you?" he asks.

"Maybe." I smile coyly up at him.

"Do you want to text Courtney or should I?" he asks.

"Text Courtney what?" she asks, walking into the living room. She plops down on the other end of the couch, looking us both over very intently.

"Think I can convince you to watch our two darling kids tonight so I can take my woman out on a date?" Matt asks her. I love how he refers to Brayden as his own. He's done it from the beginning, never has made him feel like any less than his sister.

"No convincing necessary. I was ready to kick the two of you out of here one of these nights anyway so I could get in some Auntie Court time."

"I knew I could count on you," Matt tells her as he walks over and pulls her up and into a hug.

"When was the last time she ate?" Courtney asks, nodding in Bea's direction.

"She finished maybe a half-hour ago, ate for a good solid thirty minutes, so she's nice and full."

"Perfect. Why don't you two go get ready, then, take your time showering and put on some actual makeup, do your hair, shave your legs, that kind of stuff. Then, you can feed her again before leaving and if she needs something more before you're back, I can raid the pumped stash in the fridge."

"You are a genius," Matt tells her as he pulls me up and off the couch. "Let's go get ready."

Matt pulls me down the hall and into our bedroom.

The door clicks shut, and I can tell that we won't be getting clean just yet.

"Fuck, you're beautiful," he heavily breathes out as he pulls me into him. We're standing chest-to-chest as we stare into one another's eyes.

"I'm glad that you find me beautiful when I haven't showered in multiple days, I've got a milk-stained shirt on and sweats that probably also have milk stains on them somewhere. Hopefully, no other bodily fluids, but I can't confirm or deny that right now," I ramble on.

"I don't care how many days it has been since you showered or what clothes you do or don't have on, you will always be perfect in my eyes. The incredible things this body of yours did amazes me daily. That is what I find sexy and beautiful." He leans down and kisses me, his hands cupping my cheeks like I'm the most precious thing in the world to him.

It's been weeks since we've been intimate, but there's no slowing my body's response to his touch. I am on fire and ready for him.

"Matt," I cry out as he moves his lips down my neck. His hand snakes under my shirt until he finds my hard nipple and tweaks it. "Careful, you might get soaked with milk," I warn him.

"I'm willing to take the risk," he says against my skin. Before I know it, he's got my top up and breaks away from me long enough to pull it over my head. His lips connect once again with my skin, making their way down my chest. My nursing bra follows the path of the shirt as it joins the pile. "Perfection," he murmurs, before holding my breasts together as he laps at both nipples at the same time. I can feel the tingle starting and have no way of stopping it from happening.

"Matt, it's coming," I warn him just as milk squirts him in the face.

"Surprisingly, it's sweet," he says, licking his lips.

I grab for my bra again, needing to have some pressure to stop the flow of my milk. "The not-so-glamorous side of post-partum sexy times," I tell him.

"There's nothing wrong with your body continually working to support our baby. I'll just know to avoid them, for now. I guess I can relinquish access to Bea for the time being," he says, and winks before bringing his lips to my belly. "Now, down here," he says, and trails the pads of his fingertips down my exposed belly toward my pussy, "this I won't be relinquishing to anyone."

He tugs at the waistband of my sweats, pulling them down my hips, taking my panties off with them. As soon as they fall out of his way, his tongue connects with my clit, and I just about come right that second. I rest my hands on his shoulders for some stability as his tongue slides up and down my slit. As I peek down at him on his knees, his head between my legs, I detonate. I knew it wouldn't take much for my body to come, especially this first time since giving birth.

"That didn't take long." He smirks up at me, his lips glistening with my release.

"Something tells me you won't be long, either, the first time," I toss back at him in the sassiest voice I can muster up.

"Is that so?" he asks, standing to his full height and picking me up off my feet. I wrap my legs around his waist. "Where should I fuck you first? The bed? Bent over the bathroom sink so you can watch me in the mirror as I slam my cock in and out of you?" he asks, nipping at my ear. "Or maybe in the shower, pinned up against the wall, or better yet, I can sit down on the bench, and you can ride me."

"Yes," I moan, all the options sounding like the perfect idea. "All the above," I manage to add.

Matt laughs, the low gritty sound filling our room. "My dirty-*dirty*-girl. I love it." He moves the few feet until we're standing at the edge of the bed. I slide down his body and sit on the bed. I watch as he quickly pulls his own clothes off and stands in front of me in nothing but his birthday suit.

His cock juts out, the head already turning purple with how swollen and hard he is. I lean forward and lick his tip, collecting the bead of pre-cum that was leaking from his tip with my tongue. The saltiness hits my tastebuds and it turns me on in another way. "Oh, fuck," he groans out as my lips wrap firmly around the head of his cock. I squeeze the base with a hand as I take him in deeper. I work him over, bobbing back and forth on his cock, I drive him closer to the edge.

"Okay, that's it," he grits out, pulling me off his

cock. "I want to be buried deep inside of you when I come," he says. My center pulses and I can feel my arousal.

"Yes," I tell him, agreeing with his sentiment. I flop back on the bed, opening my legs for him to step right into the opening. He circles my clit with the pad of his thumb before fisting his cock and sliding it along my slit, around my clit, and back to the opening.

"You ready?" he asks, lined up and ready to push completely inside of me.

"Yes," I pant out. The glorious stretching pain that comes with having had a few months off is present, but the full feeling has me floating on cloud nine. Matt pushes in until there's nowhere else for him to go. Once fully seated, he kisses me, slowly, at first. We build that kiss up, a tangled mess of tongue and teeth and just pure lust flowing between the two of us.

He breaks the kiss, resting his forehead against mine as his hips piston in and out. His cock making me practically see stars.

"I fucking love you," he says between thrusts. "You complete me, and I wouldn't change this for the world."

His words hit me deep. I was so worried that this would never work between us, or that I'd find him, only for him to tell me he never wanted to see me again and that he wasn't going to be in our daughter's life. Boy was I wrong.

"I love you, too," I tell him for the first time. Well, it

is the first time I've ever said the words out loud, intentionally, and directly to him. I've said it every time he's walked out the door, for months now, I've just never had the nerve to say it when he can hear. I had the fear if I gave that part of my heart to someone else again that it could be shattered like it was when Ryan died.

He kisses me hard again, my words sinking in as he gets us both to our climax.

I walk down the hall toward the sound of voices. I find Courtney in the kitchen mixing something on the counter with Brayden, while Bea is in the baby carrier strapped to her chest.

"What's happening in here?" I ask as I slip on my earrings.

Courtney looks up at me, smirking when she takes me in. "Just some cookies."

"I get to lick the spoon when we're all done!" Brayden tells me, very excitedly about that fact.

"Aunt Court is the best," I tell him, pulling him into a side hug.

"You look refreshed," she says, smirking again. "And ready to head out on the town."

"I feel human again. A shower does a girl well." I wink at her.

"Yeah, just a shower?" She laughs.

"Give me my baby so I can feed her and get out of here for a few hours. Momma needs a drink and a meal that isn't interrupted." She unclips the carrier and hands the baby over.

I take Bea into the living room and get comfortable in the recliner. She's a champion when it comes to eating, so well that she's already into the next size of clothes. It breaks my heart just how fast she's growing.

"Need anything?" Matt asks as he bends down to kiss the top of Bea's head.

"Can you refill my water bottle?" I ask.

"Of course, I can," he says, reaching for it where it's sitting empty on the end table. He gives me a chaste kiss. "Love you," he whispers.

"Love you," I whisper back. There's no missing his huge smile as he walks away to fill my water.

Once Bea is finished, I get her burped and laid down in her crib. I kiss my fingertips, then press them to her cheek before I turn the monitor on and leave her room. I stop in our bedroom to snag the other part of the monitor and turn it on so Courtney can listen for her to wake up later.

"Bea is sound asleep and in her crib. The monitor is on, and here's this part," I tell her once I'm back in the kitchen. I hand over the monitor, checking the volume so she'll hear her.

"I've got everything under control, you go have a good time, don't worry one bit about any of us," she says, shooing us out the door.

Matt reaches across the consul in his truck and slides his hand into mine, linking our fingers. He pulls our clasped hands to his lips, kissing my fingers as he drives us across town.

"You are gorgeous tonight," he says, ending the silence that had fallen between us.

"Thank you, it feels good to get dressed and put some makeup on. Thank you for thinking to do this."

"You don't have to thank me for taking you out and showing you off, I'm the lucky one in this situation."

"I don't know about that," I argue. "Where exactly are you taking me?"

"One of the steakhouses downtown. Figured a well-cooked meal would do us both good."

"I agree. I can only eat so many casseroles and leftovers. Not that I don't appreciate everyone stopping by with meals since Bea was born, but I'm burning out on them."

"I was thinking, that when the season starts again, of maybe hiring a chef to come in either daily or a couple of times a week to prep things for you that can just be put in the oven. That way, when I'm gone or on the road, it is one less thing you have to think about with the kids."

"I don't know if that is necessary, but we can discuss it," I tell him. I still don't really like it when he tries to spend money on something that I can easily do myself, although a chef does sound appealing.

"I'll wear you down," he laughs. "Or just get you to say yes when I'm buried inside you later tonight."

"Oh, is that how we're doing things now? Just remember that it's a two-way street, mister. I can ask you all sorts of shit when I've got your cock in my hand."

"Touché." He laughs.

We pull up outside the restaurant, stopping at the valet stand. My door opens and the guy offers me his hand to get down. I accept it and slide out, adjusting the hem of my dress once my feet are on the ground. "Thank you, sir," the valet says to Matt as he hands over the keys and a cash tip in exchange for the claim ticket. He slides it into his wallet and the wallet into his back pocket before escorting me with his hand on my lower back into the building.

We're greeted immediately by the hostess. "Welcome, do you have reservations this evening?" she asks.

"Yes, under Matt O'Riley," he tells her, and I don't miss the way her eyes widen and give him a good once over. On one hand, it kind of pisses me off when women do that when I'm clearly standing right next to him, but on the other hand, I understand. He's hot. I check him out every chance I get, and at the end of the day, it's me who's next to him in bed. Well, me and Bea some nights, but I'll gladly share him with her, seeing as how it was her that brought him back to me.

"Right this way," she says, smiling at him. She still hasn't acknowledged my presence at all, which is slightly comical. "Your server will be with you in just a moment," she tells him once we're seated at the table.

"Thanks," I say, making her finally gaze my way. I

can't help but flash her a sweet smile that says back off bitch, he's all mine.

"Damn, I like you a little bit jealous," Matt murmurs from next to me. His hand has found its way to my thigh, one of his favorite places to rest it when we're near each other.

"She was blatantly checking you out, wouldn't even acknowledge that I was right here until I said that," I tell him, a little offended that he isn't pissed at how she was acting.

"I paid no attention to her, you're the only one I care to check out," he tells me.

"It usually doesn't bother me, but she was a little obsessive. But let's not let it ruin our first night out without kids."

"I agree. Now, how drunk am I getting you?" he asks.

"Not drunk, just a drink. I don't want to have to pump and dump tonight."

"Damn, I was hoping for a drunk Hannah." He laughs.

Our server arrives, two glasses of ice water are balanced on his tray. "Good evening, I'm Paul, and I'll be taking care of you guys tonight. Would you like to hear tonight's specials?" he asks as he sets the glasses down in front of us.

"I think we're good with the main menu," I tell him, "but I will take a drink menu, if you have one."

"Of course, ma'am," he says, and hands over the

smaller menu. I peruse it, so many of the options sounding divine, but knowing that I need to limit myself to just one so I'm able to walk out of here tonight. It's been quite a while since I've had a drop of alcohol, maybe even as far back as my time at the resort last December.

NINETEEN
MATT

THE HOUSE IS QUIET AS I MOVE ABOUT, TUCKING A few extra presents under the tree and into the stockings. Hannah, Courtney, and I already worked on putting out all the Santa presents once the kids were in bed, but I had a few more, mostly for Hannah, that I want to be a surprise for her come morning.

I quietly make my way back to our room, stopping first to poke my head into Bea's room to check and make sure she's sleeping peacefully. When I glance down at my daughter, I'm in awe of her. The fact that I'm a dad still shocks me some days. She looks so much like her mother, which is a good thing because her mother is beautiful, inside, and out. I'm going to need to invest in some armor for when she's a teenager and boys start coming around.

"Happy first Christmas, baby girl," I whisper before pressing my kiss-laced fingers to her cheek.

I head for bed; Hannah is already sound asleep. I have a feeling that Brayden is going to have us all up before the sun comes out if his excitement at bedtime was any indication.

"Is Bea okay?" Hannah asks, half asleep as I slide in next to her. She must have thought I got up to check on the baby.

"Sound asleep," I assure her.

"Okay, love you," she says before rolling my way. Her head lands on my shoulder while her leg covers mine and her hand is flat against my chest. This is a pretty common position I find myself in most nights. One that I've come to love and crave. Whenever we're in the same room, I want her close, I want her touching me any chance I get.

"Mom, Mom, Mom," Brayden calls out from the doorway. "Santa came! Let's go!"

"Give us just a minute," she groggily says as she rolls over and sits up. Her hair is a mess, half falling out of the messy bun that she had it in last night before falling asleep.

"Okay, I'll go wake up Auntie Courtney," Brayden exclaims before dashing from the doorway.

"He's a little excited." I chuckle.

"It is Christmas morning, after all," she says, a yawn escaping her lips. I watch as she stretches, her curves on display even with my baggy T-shirt on.

"That it is," I agree.

"Holy crap, I just realized I slept all night. Did you get up with Bea at some point?" she asks.

"Nope, I checked on her when I came back to bed, but she was sound asleep. It's a Christmas miracle."

I get out of bed, stretching myself as I walk around the bed to Hannah's side. I gather her hands and pull her to her feet. "Merry Christmas, sweetheart. How about we go make our boy's morning?" I suggest.

She smiles up at me and I can't help it, I have to kiss her. "Love you," she whispers against my lips just as they connect.

"Love you, too," I tell her. I link our fingers together and lead her out of the bedroom. "Go get comfortable on the couch, I'll check on Bea and bring her to you if she's awake."

"Okay," she agrees as another yawn slips out. Looking outside, it is still dark out, so my guess is it isn't even seven AM yet.

"Good morning, baby girl," I coo at Bea. The door opening up made her stir awake, and I'm sure the empty status of her belly also attributed to that. "Let's get you a clean diaper and a full belly. You gave Mommy quite the present by sleeping all night. Who's a big girl now?" I say to her as I place her on the changing table. I grab a clean diaper and quickly change her out of the soaked one.

With Bea in my arms, we make it down the hall and find everyone waiting on us in the living room. Courtney looks just as tired as Hannah does, but they both have smiles a mile wide. I notice everyone has a present in their lap, with two more set on the couch next to Hannah.

"Come sit, then we can take turns opening up our gifts," she says, patting the cushion next to her. I don't need to be told twice, so I make my way and sit down next to her.

As soon as Bea sees her momma, she starts fussing, so I hand her over. No sense in keeping her from what she wants. I know how she feels, Hannah is our favorite person.

"Hey, sweet pea, how's my baby girl? You're such a big girl, sleeping all night for Momma," Hannah coos at her as she gets her in place and latched on to nurse.

"She must have known you wanted a full night's sleep for Christmas," Courtney comments.

"Right? Best gift ever!" Hannah says. "The only thing better would have been if I'd actually been able to sleep in."

"Can we open our presents now?" Brayden asks, his patience wearing thin.

"Go ahead, buddy, you be first," I tell him as I sit back and watch.

"Yes!" he yips out as he starts ripping the wrapping paper off the package.

"What'd you get?" I ask, leaning forward to snag the trash. It's been a long-ass time since I've been in a crazy Christmas morning present-opening session, so rookie mistake, I didn't set out any trash bags before the crazy morning started.

"It's a new switch!" He gasps and holds it up for all of us to see.

"Wow!" Hannah says, looking a little shocked. It was one of the surprise things I put out last night, so she didn't know about it.

"You must have been on the nice list, for sure," I tell Brayden as I get up to go grab some trash bags.

"Okay, Aunt Court, it's your turn," Brayden says, and turns his attention to Courtney. She tears into the wrapping, not with the level of excitement that Brayden had, but still excited, nonetheless. "What is it?" he asks once she has the box unwrapped.

"I don't know yet, I need to open the box," she tells him. I hand over a pair of scissors I also snagged from the kitchen, and she cuts through the tape on the box. "Wow!" she exclaims as she pulls the contents out. "Thank you," she says, looking my way.

"Merry Christmas," I tell her as she shifts through the items, checking them all out. I got both her and Hannah a complete package at a day spa. The ladies there packed it all up with a fluffy robe, slippers, and some at-home items so I'd have more than just the gift card to wrap up.

"Mom's turn," Brayden calls out next.

"How about Matt goes next; I'm still feeding your sister."

"Okay," he agrees easily, and turns his attention my

way. I grab the box with my name on it and rip it open. I pull out the T-shirt, holding it up to read the front, *Girl Dad.* "Perfect," I say, setting it down next to me.

We let Brayden take over opening presents until Hannah is done nursing Bea, then turn our attention to see what they both got for a few minutes. I take Bea from Hannah's arms, resting her on my chest as I pat her back until she burps.

"What'd you get, Mommy?" Brayden asks before she can get her first present open.

"Let's see," she tells him, and opens the gift he'd picked out for her to open first. "Did you make this for me?" she asks, holding up a coffee mug from one of those pottery places where you can go in and paint your own items.

"Yep! Auntie Court took me!" he tells her.

"It's perfect! I love it, thank you."

"You're welcome," he says before turning back to the pile of presents still to open.

"Are you ready for your stocking?" I ask, ready for her to see what I snuck into it last night.

"Sure," Hannah agrees, giving me a sweet smile. I steal a chaste kiss before standing up. I place Bea in her swing, as she's back asleep with her full belly, before getting the stockings down. I hand all of them out, then take my place next to her on the couch again.

"Matt," she gasps, and I know she's found the box.

I slide off the couch, kneeling in front of her as I reach for her hand and the box.

"Hannah," I say her name, but have to stop to clear my throat, the emotions of the moment catching up with me. "Hannah, we met by chance just over a year ago. Fate wanted that chance meeting to be more, and here we are, a beautiful baby girl, your son, and the two of us living as a happy family. I knew long ago that you were my forever, would you marry me and make me your forever?" I ask as I pull the ring out of the box.

She looks between the box and me, tears already streaming down her face. I reach up and wipe them away with my free hand as I wait for her answer. "Yes," she finally says.

"Way to make the man wait for the answer," Courtney calls out from her seat.

I slide the ring on her finger and lean in to press my lips to hers. "I love you."

"I love you, too," she says before gazing back at the ring on her finger.

"She said yes, buddy! We're getting married," I turn to Brayden and tell him.

He whoops, excitement showing all over his face.

"Does that mean I can start calling you Dad, now?" he asks and I almost collapse at his question. Knowing that he thinks of me as his dad is the best gift—outside of his mother saying yes, and the birth of his sister—I could be given.

"If it's okay with your mom and you want to call me Dad, I'd be honored to be that to you," I tell him as I pull him in for a hug.

"Crap, I didn't expect to cry so much this morning," Courtney says, trying to bring some humor into the room.

"Me either," Hannah agrees with her. I look at both of them, and they're both wiping at falling tears, thankfully, they're all happy ones.

"How about some breakfast?" Hannah suggests a few minutes later. There are still a few presents left to be opened, but all the big ones are done.

"Can we have French toast?" Brayden asks.

"Sure can," I tell him as I scoop him up and toss him over my shoulder. We head for the kitchen. I set him down on the edge of the island then turn to start getting out everything we'll need to make a Christmas breakfast feast.

TWENTY

HANNAH

7 MONTHS LATER

I bounce Bea on my legs as we sit in the family suite of the stadium waiting for the players to be announced. She's sporting the cutest little outfit, her daddy's number on her back, but instead of O'Riley where his name goes, it says Daddy. Brayden is sporting the same design on his T-shirt that he proudly wears to every game.

"Hey, how's it going?" Riley asks as she takes the seat next to me, her son and daughter trailing behind her.

"Good, how are you? You look a little frazzled."

"Oh, you know how it is, kids make me late to everything," she says, turning to make sure her kids are not getting into any trouble.

"Are you sure it isn't because that husband of yours can't keep his hands off of you and knocked you up again and everything makes you puke?" Jillian smirks. I think she's the only person that could get away with talking to her like that, seeing as how they're sisters-in-law.

"You mean, the exact way my brother is with you?" She smirks right back. My eyes bounce back and forth between the two women like a ping-pong ball does in a match.

"Wait, does that mean you're both expecting again?" I ask, making sure I didn't miss the subtle hints.

"You caught that, did you?" Jillian asks, smiling over at me.

"Congratulations, how exciting! Cousins that will be the same age."

"I swear we didn't plan this, it just happened," Riley tells me.

"Even if you did, babies are always a gift."

"That they are," Riley says as she takes Bea's hand. "What about you guys, are you going to try for any more?"

"I always wanted a houseful, and I know Matt would like at least one more. Maybe we can start trying after the wedding."

"How are things coming along with that?" Jillian asks.

"Good. I met with the planner just yesterday and we went over so much. It's all coming together perfectly."

"Oh, good! If you need anything, you know where to find me," she offers.

"Thanks. I still need to nail down a baker. The one I thought we were going to go with ended up not being available for our date, so that is my priority this week."

"Oh, I know of the perfect bakery. I found her on Instagram," Riley says, pulling her phone out. "I had her make Evie's cake and it was the best thing I've ever tasted."

"I do remember that. I'll definitely message her to see what she says," I tell her, checking out her Instagram feed.

Our attention is pulled to the field, where the team is being introduced. As each of the guys runs out and lines up on the baseline, the volume in the stadium rises with the cheers of the fans. I love seeing all the support the guys get. As reigning champions, and one hell of a season under their belts so far this year, the games have all been sellouts, even the mid-week daytime games, which is impressive.

The kids and I stand outside the locker room at the end of the game, waiting for Matt to come out so we can all go home. There are other family members, staff from the team and stadium, as well as media milling around, which is pretty normal, especially after a win. Every time the door to the locker room opens, it is funny to watch the media all perk up, hoping to get another sound bite from one of the players, only to be disappointed when it isn't a player or the player they were hoping for.

"There's Dad!" Brayden exclaims when Matt steps out of the locker room a few minutes later. His eyes immediately find mine, and the smile on his face tells me that he heard Brayden. I still get all mushy the way he responds to Brayden calling him Dad.

We start walking toward one another, meeting in the middle. He picks Brayden up, swinging him in his arms like he weighs nothing. I can't do that quite so easily now that he's growing up so much.

"How are my girls?" he asks, dipping down to kiss the top of Bea's head as she sleeps peacefully on my chest. His lips find mine, next, for a quick kiss.

"Good, tired, and ready to go home."

"Mr. O'Riley, can I get a quick interview?" a woman calls out to him. He looks at me, asking with his eyes if I'm okay with the delay. I give him a quick nod, knowing that this is part of his job and a necessity sometimes.

"Sure, a quick question or two and then I need to get my family home," he tells her.

Bea starts fussing in my arms, so I miss the questions and his answers as I try and soothe her back to sleep.

"Did that go okay?" I ask as we walk toward the exit and into the players' parking lot.

"Yeah, just the normal how'd I feel tonight, what do I think our chances of back-to-back-to-back pennant wins kind of questions. I swear they already have my answers to those questions in a thousand sound bites, but they always want new ones."

"Always trying to one-up each other and hoping that you'll mess up and say something new that they can be the ones to report first on."

"Are you sure you're not the one that has dealt with the press for the last decade?" he teases.

We make it home, both kids are now passed out in the back seat. I grab Bea's carrier while Matt carries Brayden inside and to his room.

We've become quite the team, dividing and conquering so that we can get both kids into bed and still have a little bit of time to spend together without them pulling us in different directions.

"Do you want a glass of wine?" Matt asks as he comes down the hall, heading for the kitchen.

"Sure, but only if you're having one, as well," I tell him as I relax on the couch.

He comes in a few minutes later, two stemless wine glasses in hand. He hands me one, then clinks glasses with mine in a mock cheers' movement.

"Did you know that both JJ and Derek have knocked up their wives again?" I ask him.

"I found out tonight," he says before taking a drink of his wine. "I told them I won't be long behind them, hopefully."

"You didn't." I smack his chest, sitting up to stare him down.

"Something wrong with that statement?" He smirks and raises his brows at me. "I'd get you pregnant tonight if I thought you'd go along with it."

"I need a few more months of sleeping all night, and maybe a few more of a baby that isn't nursing before I'll be ready to start all over," I tell him honestly. "As much as I love the first year, it is fucking draining on me. I'm not getting any younger, so each time it gets that much harder."

"I can appreciate that need to wait, but when you're ready, you know where to find me. Until then, we'll just have fun practicing," he says, and pulls me in for a kiss.

"Lots of practicing," I say against his lips.

"What do you say we go practice now?" he asks hopefully.

"I could probably be talked into some sexy times."

"No talking necessary," Matt says, and he takes my wine glass and sets it on the end table before scooping me up in his arms and carrying me down the hall to our room.

Matt sets me on the bed and steps back. He strips out of all his clothes. I love his body. How toned he keeps it, like a freaking work of art. It's kind of disgusting how few hours he actually spends in the gym and still looks this damn good.

"Like something you see, sweetheart?" He smirks at me. My eyes flick to his cock and a coy smile tugs at my lips. His cock jerks at the attention. A moan falls from my lips as he reaches down and grips his length in his fist. He shuttles it up and down the shaft, circling around his swollen head, collecting the bead of pre-cum that has leaked out.

"Mhmm," I hum, and can feel my panties getting wetter as the minutes tick by while I watch him pleasure himself.

"Strip," he commands. I don't stall, tugging my tank-top off, my bra quickly following it. I have to slide off the bed and stand up to take my jeans and panties off, which doesn't take long when I'm motivated to do so.

As soon as I'm naked, Matt has me flat on my back and is kissing up my inner thigh. My body quivers in anticipation of where his lips will land next as he slowly pushes me up the bed, following with his own body as he lays out on the bed between my legs.

"Someone's wet for me," he murmurs as his fingers slide easily through my folds. "Have you been a good girl?" he asks, and slides a finger inside me, quickly finding a sensitive spot that has my eyes rolling back in my head. "Or a bad girl that needs to be punished?" he asks, and slaps my clit. The sting of pain is quickly covered by the lapping of his tongue. He fucks me good with his fingers, never releasing contact on my clit as he drives me wild as I chase my orgasm.

"Fuck, Matt, I'm so close," I tell him between panted breaths. "So close." I grab hold of his hair as I grind my pussy against his face. I don't want him to move I'm so close.

His fingers are working overtime as I build and build. He releases my clit, but only long enough to blow air directly on the very sensitive bundle of nerves, followed by quick flicks of his tongue before he sucks it back between his lips.

That's all it takes; I crash over the edge of my orgasm. My body going rigid before it goes completely limp.

I feel him slide up and lay down next to me. My mind is swimming in my blissful state, for the moment. I start to come to when I feel his lips coasting over my skin, leaving little kisses and love bites in tender areas.

"Are you ready for me?" he asks, hovering over the top of me now. His cock shuttles over my clit and the sensitive bundle perks right back to life, ready for round two.

He doesn't need words from me, I just pull him in for a searing kiss as he pushes his cock inside of me, inch by incredible inch.

Matt

I PUSH INSIDE HANNAH, HER GASPS OF PLEASURE fueling me on as I make love to her. I feel the most at home when I'm buried deep inside her body.

Every ache and pain, every moment of self-doubt is drowned out when we're connected like this. I roll my hips, hitting each and every one of her trigger spots as I methodically swivel, speeding up or slowing down based on the moans that fall from her lips. I've learned this woman's incredible body, what she likes and doesn't. It is always my goal to find out something new without going overboard.

"That's it, baby, your pussy gripping my cock feels so good. Make me come, baby," I tell her. "Fuck, scratch those nails into my back," I encourage as she does just that.

"Matt!" she cries out. "Don't stop," she instructs. No way am I stopping now. Her pussy grips me tightly, so I hitch a leg up higher on my hip and piston my hips. Our bodies are making all sorts of noises as they slap together, sweat covering every inch.

"Yes!" Hannah yells as she falls over the edge, her orgasm racking her body hard. The convulsions and tightening of her pussy pushes me over the edge, my own taking hold and ravishing my body as I empty everything I have into her.

I collapse, pinning her to the bed beneath me until I can think enough to roll us over. My cock slides out when we do, and I instantly miss the connection.

We lay there, basking in all the sex hormones, our hearts beating together as we automatically were pulled together, almost like we're magnets that are only activated when the other is around.

"Are you still awake?" I ask, not sure if she is due to how calm her breathing is.

"Somewhat," she says.

"There was one question the reporter asked me today, one that I've never answered until now," I tell her a bit nervously. I get asked a lot about my "instant family" and after confirming I did, in fact, have a girlfriend—now fiancée—and she was a single mom, and we had a kid on the way at the time, I haven't really answered any questions that pertained to my personal life. Hannah and the kids didn't sign up to be a professional baseball player or the spotlight that brings. Yes, Hannah knew that was my job and my life when she agreed to be in it, but that doesn't mean that I can't shield them from it as much as I possibly can.

"What was that?" she asks, propping her chin up on my chest so we can look at each other.

"She asked me what had changed, why my play was different, more calculated, and precise."

"Okay, and what did you tell her?" she asks.

"I told her it was you. My change up. My good luck charm."

"Why do you think that?" she asks.

"Hannah, fate might have brought us together, but the love we've built as a family has been the true game changer. One that I never saw coming that first day on the beach when I stopped to toss the ball with Brayden. I wouldn't change how we met, or the events in the days after, because if it wasn't for that one magical night together, we might not have all the nights of our forever to go. I love you more than I can ever express, and I thank my lucky stars every day that you came into my life and threw the change up I never knew I needed, but so desperately wanted."

EPILOGUE

HANNAH

WE SIT AROUND THE LIVING ROOM, THE HOUSE IS decked out for Christmas. All my favorite people fill the room as we make memories to last a lifetime.

"Can I get you a refill?" Matt asks, his lips brushing across my temple.

"Yes, please," I answer before stealing a quick kiss from him.

I can't help but watch him as he walks away. I pinch myself every so often, making sure that this is my real life. That I lucked out in finding love not once, but twice in my lifetime.

"For my bride," he says, handing over the glass of ice water. We've been married a little over two months now, so he takes every opportunity to refer to me as his bride.

"Thank you, husband," I say, accepting the glass. He takes a seat next to me, tugging me into his side.

I glance around at all that is going on. Matt's mom is on the floor playing with Bea and one of her many toys, while Brayden is showing Matt's dad a Lego set he got a few weeks ago that he proudly built all by himself.

"What do we think about opening one present each tonight?" I call out to the room at large.

Everyone quiets down, looking over at me for a few seconds before the room grows loud again from all the chatter.

"Brayden, how about you find a present for everyone," I suggest. He happily hops up and starts pulling presents out for everyone to open.

My anxiety is growing as the minutes pass. I can't wait for Matt to open up the box Brayden has handed him. I'll have to wait, as we start with the kids, letting them open up the new Christmas pajamas I ordered, along with a new Christmas book.

Matt's parents each open a small gift, a frame that Brayden decorated for each of them, along with a picture of him with them.

"Oh, Brayden," Christie gasps, taking in the gift. She pulls him into a hug and my own heart melts at how his parents just accepted us right into the fold of their family. They think of Brayden as their grandson, just as they see Bea as their granddaughter. "I love it." She kisses his cheek before releasing him again.

"Dad, you next!" Brayden calls out, standing up and coming over to the couch.

"Okay, do you want to help me?" he asks him. Matt moves the box off his legs, pulling Brayden into his lap. I couldn't have planned this better if I tried. I glance over at Courtney and see that she's already got her phone out and is recording for me.

"You do it," Brayden tells Matt as he hands the box back to him.

I bite on my bottom lip, willing him to open the box faster. He finally tears off all the paper, pushing it aside before opening the top of the box. He pulls out the packet of papers and starts to read the top one out loud.

"Congratulations. Attached you will find all the documents required to process your application for adoption for Brayden L. Knight." He stops reading, looking at me and then down at Brayden, tears already falling down his cheeks. "Are you serious?" he finally gets out.

"Yes," I say, already nodding my head yes as tears run down my cheeks.

"Hell yes!" he exclaims, hugging Brayden to him tightly.

"You'll officially be my dad now," Brayden says as his smile takes over his face.

"Oh, buddy, I'll be more than happy to be your forever dad," Matt tells him. His words squeeze my heart just a little bit tighter.

"We're so happy for you," Christie chimes in. I survey the room and notice that not one of the adults in the room has a dry eye.

"I got all of it," Courtney says as she taps at the screen of her phone. Moments later, my own phone chimes and I see she's airdropping the video to me.

"Thank you for getting that," I tell her as I accept the video.

"Of course, now no more making me cry. It's Christmas Eve, for goodness sake, we need some non-crying happy moments."

"How about some hot chocolate and a Christmas movie?" Christie suggests.

"Can I have extra marshmallows?" Brayden asks, perking up at the idea.

"I suppose Nana can sneak you a few extra." She winks at him and holds out her hand for him to take so they can head into the kitchen and start making the drinks.

Matt pulls me into his arms, his nose buried in the crook of my neck. "Thank you," he whispers, only for me to hear.

"It was all Brayden's idea. He asked me about it just before the wedding. I called the lawyer that JJ and Riley used, and he got everything drawn up. It was fairly easy, since Ryan isn't alive, so there was no waiting for parental rights to be signed away or anything like that."

"I promise I'll always think of him as my own, not that I'll push Ryan's memory out, but in my mind, he's no less special to me than Bea or any future kids we might have will be to me."

"I know, and that's why I was fully on board with his request, but just know that he wants this just as badly as you do. He loves you."

"I love him," he says, the emotion choking him up. "So damn much."

"About those future kids," I whisper, and he sits up abruptly, looking me dead in the eyes.

"Are we," he begins to ask, his eyes dropping to my stomach before coming back up to my eyes.

All I have to do is nod, my smile breaking out. His lips crash into mine, kissing me hard.

"Get a room," Courtney calls out from her recliner. "There are kids around," she chuckles.

Matt pulls back, glancing her way and shooting her what I fear is a death glare by the way she cracks up.

"It's good for them to see their parents loving one another," he says matter-of-factly. "Plus, if I want to make out with my wife in my own home, I'm damn sure going to do it."

"Yeah, yeah," she mutters. "Damn honeymoon stage."

"Don't worry, Courtney, we'll find you a nice guy who will sweep you off your feet," he tells her.

"Don't be promising something you can't fulfill," she warns.

"Challenge accepted." He smirks.

I slide into bed a few hours later, the house is quiet and we're ready for the crazy morning in just a few short hours.

Matt's arms wrap around me, pulling me in close to his warm body. "When did you test and find out?" he asks, nuzzling my neck and turning me on.

"This morning," I say as I shift my neck to give him better access.

"I should have known something was up when you turned down the wine for water," he says as I roll over to face him.

"I wanted to tell you, but also keep it a secret from everyone else."

"How are you feeling?"

"Fine, just a little bit tired. My boobs are a bit tender."

"Fine enough for me to do this?" he asks before sliding down my body, dropping open-mouth kisses along the way. He lifts my tank-top up, exposing my breasts to him. He's ever so gentle, lapping and kissing rather than biting and sucking.

His fingers trail down my body, slipping into my panties and finding my already swollen clit. "Matt," I cry out as he pinches it before sliding two fingers inside of me.

"That's it, beautiful, come for me, ride my hand," he instructs. He slides lower, pushing my panties down with his free hand. He circles my clit with his tongue before sucking it in his mouth. Between his fingers inside me and his mouth on my bundle of nerves, I detonate, falling right over the orgasm cliff.

I feel the loss of his fingers when he pulls them out,

but am quickly filled again, this time with his hard cock. He pumps into me, my body pulsing around his girth. His strokes prolong my pleasure as my orgasm rolls on and on.

"Fuck, baby, yes, squeeze my cock. Just like that. Be a good girl and make me come." His dirty words spur me on as I take every thrust he gives me.

I run my hands down his back, my nails leaving marks as they go. "I'm going to come again," I warn him as I feel my body starting to spasm once again.

His body slams into me, his orgasm taking hold as he goes rigid on top. The pulsing of his cock sets my own orgasm off, and we fall into ecstasy together.

Once we've both caught our breath, he pushes up until he's hovering over me. "I fucking love you, more than I can ever put into words. You make me the happiest I've ever been. Thank you for this life you've given me," he says before kissing me tenderly.

"I think I'm the one that should be thanking you. You came into my life when I didn't really know what life had in store for me. I knew I had it in me to love again, but you showed me what that really entailed. I couldn't have asked for a better man than you are. The way you stepped right into a dad role with Brayden. The way you automatically embraced the miracle we created together, and now our life today with another baby on the way. We really have created something beautiful together, and I can't wait to see how life unfolds for us over the next sixty years.

READY FOR SOME MORE BASEBALL? START BACK AT the beginning with Derek and Jillian in The Perfect Pitch!

Ryker

San Francisco Shockwaves Book 1
May 19, 2022
Pre-Order on your favorite retailer!
Add on Goodreads today!

Nothing Bundt Forever

Sweet Valley, Tennessee Book 2
July 27, 2022
Pre-order on your favorite retailer!
Add on Goodreads today!

ALSO BY SAMANTHA LIND

Indianapolis Eagles Series

Just Say Yes ~ Scoring The Player

Playing For Keeps ~ Protecting Her Heart

Against The Boards ~ The First Intermission

The Hardest Shot ~ The Game Changer

Rookie Move ~ The Final Period

Box Set 1 {Books 1-3} ~ Box Set 2 {Books 4-6}

Indianapolis Lightning Series

The Perfect Pitch ~ The Curve Ball

The Screw Ball ~ The Change Up

Lyrics & Love Series

Marry Me ~ Drunk Girl

Rumor Going 'Round ~ Just A Kiss

Standalone Titles

Tempting Tessa

Until You ~ An Aurora Rose Reynolds Happily Ever
Alpha Crossover Novella

Until Her Smile ~ An Aurora Rose Reynolds Happily

Ever Alpha Crossover Novel

Cocky Doc ~ A Cocky Hero Club Novel

Nothing Bundt Love

SAN FRANCISCO SHOCKWAVES

Ryker

Aiden

ACKNOWLEDGMENTS

I have so many people to thank that I sometimes don't know where to start. I'll start with my family. Thank you for encouraging me to write all these stories that keep me up at night. Thank you for all the time you give me to hide away and type all the words!

Renee - I seriously couldn't do this without you! It is crazy sometimes how alike we think!

My multiple author group chats - Procrastinating & Butt Stuff, Chat full of Mommies, OG Girls - Thank you for all the laughs, sprints, and words of encouragement.

My readers! You are the real MVPs here! Thank you for reading my books and loving my characters just as much as I do. I can't believe this is the end of another amazing series, one that has taken my author career to another level. I'm sad to be leaving these guys, yet so excited to see what the future has in store!

xoxo,

Samantha

ABOUT THE AUTHOR

Samantha Lind is a contemporary romance author. Having spent the first 27 years of her life in Alaska, she now calls Las Vegas home, where she lives with her husband and two sons. She enjoys spending time with her family, traveling, reading, watching hockey (Go Knights Go!), and listening to country music.

Connect with Samantha in the following places:
www.samanthalind.com
samantha@samanthalind.com

Reader Group
Samantha Lind's Alpha Loving Ladies
Good Reads
https://goo.gl/t3R9Vm
Newsletter
https://bit.ly/FDSLNL

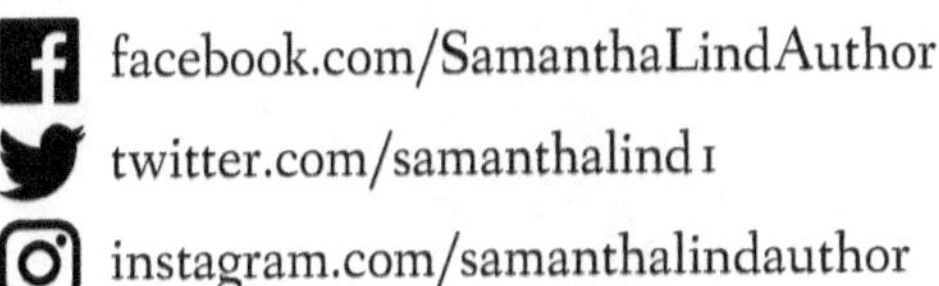
facebook.com/SamanthaLindAuthor
twitter.com/samanthalind1
instagram.com/samanthalindauthor

www.ingramcontent.com/pod-product-compliance
Lightning Source LLC
Chambersburg PA
CBHW032157190726
48289CB00007BA/2272